Shadow's Moon

Season Four

Shadow's Moon Season Four
Ash Rock Series
Copyright © 2023 By Marcelle Valentine

Contact information: marcellevalentine.com/

Published in the United States of America by Medusa Publishing.
Medusa Publishing is a registered trade name of Medusa Publishing, LLC.

First Edition: 2023

Reading a book is like meeting a new friend.

Shadow's Moon

Ash Rock Series
Marcelle Valentine

 Medusa Publishing

Contents

Episode Eighty-Six: Never Goodbye

Brady

I DON'T KNOW how it's possible my best friend, the one man I learned I could trust more than my own family, is dead from my actions. Had I not challenged Travis, Colt never would have had to intervene. He would not have been stabbed by the cowards who sit as Alpha and Beta of my pack. While I'm certain Travis and Max would never have allowed me to walk off pack lands alive, Colt may have. Now he's dead, Maggie is heartbroken, and I don't know how to make any of this shit better.

Foster and Shay have done everything in their power to make me feel welcome and at home here, but I can never rest until the assholes who did this to him are dead.

Foster had to stop me from leaving on more than one occasion to exact my revenge. The first time was the day I woke up and Shay delivered the heart-wrenching news he was gone. That day Foster told me if I wanted to leave, I had to get past him first. If I could beat him, then he wouldn't stop me. To say the least, it was a feeble attempt on my part. Foster subdued me easily with one arm. He was right; I was in no condition to avenge Colton, but make no mistake, I will kill the assholes who ended his life.

When I arrived at the ridge where Foster told me I would find Maggie, I discovered a vastly different person than the woman she was a few weeks ago. The marks remained visible around her throat from the collar they put on her. As do the lash marks I can barely see around her shirt collar. Shay told me she refused to leave Colton's side. A constant vigil with her praying to the Moon Goddess he would recover. She waited for days until the night he took his last breath and silently slipped away.

Maggie's heart broke, and she has remained on the ridge since then, refusing to come in, refusing food, refusing their help. I understand her position. She lost the man she loved, and as painful as it was for me, I can't imagine how terrible losing him had to be on her. So I did the only thing I could. I did it as her Alpha; I did it for my beta, but mostly I did it as her friend... I held her as she broke down and cried for hours for the man we both lost.

Today is the day we finally lay him to rest. He should be with his family, but I know this is no longer an option. So here, among the people who cared for him as he slipped away from this world, will have to do. Once again, Foster proves what makes him a good Alpha and a better man. He arranged the funeral of a man he met once and treated him as though he had been a member of this pack his entire life. We honor him not only as a fallen shifter but as the beta he so proudly became.

"I am aware most of you never had the opportunity to get to know Colton. For those of you who did not, you will never understand how unfortunate this is. Colt was a great man, an honorable beta, quick to offer a helping hand, and the best friend anyone could ever hope for. But for those who knew him, we would also say he was funny and trustworthy. He didn't know the word quit. When he loved, he did it wholeheartedly, and he loved you, Maggie. Colt told me as much. Told me he didn't need to find his mate because he found his heart when he found you." Maggie tries unsuccessfully to stifle the sob she has been holding in, and as suspected, Shay is there to comfort her.

"I will never be able to express how much I appreciate what you all did to help him. I know Colt would say the same if he could. You all are a testament to what a pack should be, and Foster is the epitome of the kind of Alpha everyone who carries the title should strive to become. Thank you for your kindness and sympathy. I hope one day I can repay it." I turn to place my hand on Colton's coffin; this part is for him alone. "I'll spend the rest of my life regretting that my actions caused this. I love you, brother. This is not goodbye; it's until I see you again."

Foster and his friends act as Colt's last honor guard as we carry him to where he will rest until time and space erase us from existence. The howls from the sentinels lining the ridge drift on the winds to inform the shifter community of our loss.

After the ceremony, Foster hugs me before instructing everyone to give Maggie and me a second alone.

"He would have hated all the attention," Maggie says as she places the flowers on his grave.

"Yeah."

"I can picture his red face."

11

"I don't think I have ever seen another guy who blushed as much as he did."

"He would have told you you got one thing wrong in your speech," she whispers.

"What's that?"

"He would have told you he didn't always offer a helping hand. He was ashamed of himself for treating Shay as he did and for not stepping in to stop the rest of the pack. It's the one thing he told me he would never forgive himself for."

"He shouldn't be ashamed." Shay's soft voice interjects.

"Colt told me his one regret was never expressing how sorry he was before you left, and if it was the last thing he did, he wanted to apologize."

"Colton doesn't owe me anything. He never did. He may not have stopped the other pack members, but he was never outright mean to me."

"Despite that, it was something he felt he owed you, and since he can no longer ask for it," Maggie's eyes fill with tears as her lip quivers. Shay does not hesitate to wrap her arms around her. After several minutes, Maggie pulls away to wipe her eyes so she could finish what she felt Shay needed to hear.

"Since he can no longer ask for your forgiveness, I'll do it for him... Shay, please forgive him for ever making you feel like you didn't matter. For every time he pretended like he wasn't helping you, for not standing up for you as he knew he should. Forgive him so he can forgive himself and rest in peace."

"Of course, I forgive him. But, as I previously stated, he never needed to ask because he didn't do—"

"We all did you wrong, Shay. Every member of the pack. So, Colton isn't the only one who should be asking for your forgiveness."

"Please stop. I left that life behind me. Besides, I'm happy here. I know the ones who regret what happened, and I forgive you... Even Sadie," she says with a laugh. "I'm sorry we couldn't help him."

"That's not your fault. It's Travis and Max's. A mistake I will make them pay dearly for." This declaration is equal parts promise to my fallen friend and a threat to the ones who killed him.

Episode Eighty-Seven: Foster's Going to Kill Me

Shay

KEEPING BRADY HERE while he heals when he only wants to avenge Colt's death is a workout. Foster, Denver, and Atlas are the only ones who can stop him. On the night of Colton's funeral, poor Finch finds out the hard way Brady is not a slouch when it comes to fighting. With Foster attending pack business, I discovered Brady hitchhiking. His destination was Montana. His goal was to kill Travis and Max. Every time he put his thumb up, I grabbed his hand before waving the car by. When reason didn't work, I called Finn.

Finch must have shifted because he was there in a couple of minutes. Like me, he told him that seeking vengeance now would not work out in his favor. It escalated to a physical altercation when he realized Brady was too irate to listen to reason.

Finch held his own for several minutes until Brady decided we had detained him long enough and knocked Finch out with one punch. Luck must have been on my side because, as Finn flopped, Atlas pulled up next to us. When Brady tried to deal with Atlas the same way he had Finch, he found out the hard way Atlas does not go down so easily. In fact, Brady, not Atlas, ends up on his ass. Followed by Atlas tossing him in the back seat next to a mumbling Finch before he delivers all of us back to a fuming Foster.

It took me a few minutes to understand Finch and Brady were not the only two who pissed him off. It seems I earned a piece of his ire too. When I questioned why he was mad at me, he told me anytime I was in trouble, my first call should always be to him, no one else. Finch's black eye and dislocated shoulder lasted longer than Foster's frustration with me after I showed him how sorry I was.

Foster dealt with Brady differently than any of us thought he would. Instead of yelling at him or knocking him on his ass, Foss hugged him. Brady was as shocked by his response as Finch and I, but he returned his embrace when Foster swore they would not let what Travis or Max did to him stand. Foss confirmed Colton's sacrifice would not go unanswered. He promised Brady he was only waiting to give Brady a chance to regain his full strength, and then Foster did something that stunned us all; he called him brother.

"Hey, Brady," I yell through the open window as I drive up next to him when I find him jogging down the road.

"Hey, Shay," he parrots back but comes over to lean in the window. Brady looks good. It took some time, but he's finally gaining back some of the weight he lost when he fought for his life, and after waking to the news of Colt's death, which sent him spiraling into a pit of self-blame and despair.

"Want to go for a ride with me?"

"Depends," he tells me with a mischievous grin.

"On what?"

"On where you are going and if lunch is included."

I can't help the eye roll or the grin I give him. "Lunch is a definite because I'm starving. Where I'm going is to pick up Ness from the bus station." He doesn't respond, but since he practically dove through my window, I would have to say he's going, which causes me to laugh.

"What? You had me at lunch, babydoll."

"You better watch that babydoll shit if you don't want a hotheaded Alpha up your ass."

"If you are referring to my brother...." Hearing him call Foster his brother warms my heart. I like it, but I think they like it too. "then I have no fear. In case you haven't heard, we're tighter than a nun's—"

"You don't have to finish your thought. Thanks for the image though."

"It's what I'm here for."

"So, how's training going?"

"Your boyfriend is hardcore."

"What, he's your brother when he's cool, but when Foss is in ass-kicking Alpha mode, he's my boyfriend?" I ask with a laugh.

"Now you're getting it," he confirms as he ruffles my hair. "Seriously, it's good he's helping me regain my strength and taught me some new fighting techniques."

"I think he learned some of them from Atlas."

"What the hell is the deal with that guy? I swear to the goddess, when I hit him, it was like punching a fucking brick wall. Actually, I think the wall has more give than that guy does."

"I don't know. I haven't figured it out yet. The only thing I can say is Atlas and Denver don't appear to be normal."

"You think?" he responds with a laugh. "Because I'm willing to bet they're not human." Even though shifters have a gene that allows us to morph our bodies into our animal counterparts, we still consider ourselves human. Supernatural but human all the same.

"Imagine if it was Denver you hit."

"Hard pass. I don't want to shatter every bone in my hand, and something tells me I should expect nothing less if I punch that big ass gorilla."

We filled the rest of the ride with light conversation. It's the first time I don't feel guilty choosing Foster over Brady, but I think it's because Brady realizes how much I care about Foster. I could use the L word because, in reality, I love him; however, neither of us has ever said it, and I certainly don't want to be the first, let alone admit it to someone else.

Because I hate being late for anything, our lunch includes a few fast food burgers and flat pop. I owe him a better lunch soon.

"So where did this Ness go?"

"She left to help the sister pack of Ash Rock. It's where Foster's best friend is."

"What happened?"

"Nothing major. Their salutary went to visit his family. Ness volunteering to go there was precautionary only."

"Is she anything like her cousins?"

"Better. She's a perfect cross between the two." We only have to wait a short time before the bus carrying Ness pulls up. Jumping out of Foster's truck, I rush over to greet her.

She smiles at Brady as he slowly approaches. "Nice to see you up and about."

Everything shifts the second he takes her hand in his. It's like the world stops moving for them, and I admit I'm slightly confused by Brady's comment when I hear him say, "Oh shit, Foster is going to fucking kill me."

But Ness's response removes any doubt about what happened when she says one word, "Mate."

Episode Eighty-Eight: Mistake the Goddess Made

Foster

"*Y*OU HAVE TWO fucking seconds to correct what you just said."

Brady steps in front of Ness, shielding her from any perceived harm, and declares with more conviction than most would have when confronting two pissed-off shifters, "Ness is my mate. I'm sorry if you dislike it, but regardless of whether you like it or not, it changes nothing."

The low growl from Finch and I confirms the latter is where our feelings lie. If it were not for my mate standing between the man I want to knock on his ass and me, he would understand the last time he witnessed me fight; I did so only half-heartedly.

"Nessie, step away from this asshole."

"Damn it, Finn, stop calling me—"

"Vanessa. Get. Away. From. Him." Finch demands. I have never witnessed my cousin be this forceful with her. Most of the time, he doesn't get involved leaving her to make her own decisions. Or at least this is what she believes because we have already ensured Ness's safety from behind the scenes. Any guy who wants to date Ness has to go through Finch and me first.

"No."

"What the hell do you mean no?" I snap, trying to move around Shay.

"Foster, three hours ago, you were calling him your brother. Now you want to kill him because of something beyond his control. The Moon Goddess declared them mates, not Brady, not Ness, the Goddess. No different than she proclaimed we are." Shay's attempt to halt the inevitable fight brewing between us is noble, if not misplaced.

"She's not you, and he's not me."

"Stop this nonsense, Foster. You're getting all worked up over nothing," Ness yells as she pushes past Brady. My cousin's impatience is clearly winning out since she is tapping her foot with enough zeal I can feel the effect over here.

"How the hell can you call this nothing, Ness?"

"Because I don't know if I want a mate." Her admission silences the room and brings everything to a screeching halt. Is she lying to save the man behind her, or are we about to relive the same bullshit mistake I made?

Not to mention Brady's face, which has been turning a dark shade of red until Ness's declaration turns it ashen. If I had to guess, the red had nothing to do with embarrassment and everything to do with his irritation, and now the lack of color is him realizing he is on the verge of losing the mate he only found a few hours ago.

*****

Leading Ness into my office, I close the door behind us so we can have a candid conversation. One in which she can tell me what the hell is going on.

"Not that I'm trying to persuade you to accept the bond and announce yourself his mate, but Ness, we all witnessed how well it worked out for me trying to deny what the Goddess deemed to be. So why don't you tell me your reasons for not wanting a mate?"

Ness exhales through pursed lips prior to shuffling over to plop in the chair across the desk from me. I wait patiently, granting her all the time she needs to answer my lingering questions. Her eyes shift from one unimportant object to the next, never looking at me. I know this will not be a brief conversation when she nibbles on her lower lip.

"Ness?"

Calling her name only causes her to replace her lip with her thumbnail. A clear sign she is conflicted.

"Ness." My tone is less questioning and more quiet encouragement.

"I'm afraid she made a mistake. How could the Moon Goddess give me a mate that could treat Shay the way he did? A man who could quietly stand by while they tormented her. To be so unwilling to step in or end their actions. Shay's the sweetest person I know, and he let them torture her. How could I accept a mate who shares the same blood as the miserable prick you had to kill? Tell me how I'm supposed to look past any of these things, Foss?"

I walk around the desk to kneel in front of her. "Damn, little Ness, that's a lot of doubt."

21

"I think it's warranted."

"Let me ask you a question." She looks at me, hoping whatever question I might ask will provide her with the answers she seeks. "Do you love me?"

"That's a stupid question. Of course I do. You're like my brother."

"Shouldn't you hate me?"

"How could you ask me something like that, Foss?"

"The same blood you fault Brady for having also flows through my veins. So if you hate him for it, then by default, you must also hate me. Not to mention the hell I put my mate through."

"I could never hate you. Besides, you are nothing like the pricks who hurt Shay."

"And as much as I hate to admit this, neither is Brady."

"I think the world may be coming to an end."

"Yeah-yeah, listen, Ness, the decision is yours to make, but I can tell you refusing to acknowledge your mate is one of the hardest things I ever had to do." Especially if you like breathing because as much as she steals my breath away each time I catch a glimpse of her now, denying her was like refusing the oxygen necessary for life. "Don't make your choice based on a man he had no control over."

"Okay, well, what about the way he treated Shay? Surely you can't be okay with that?" she asks while leaning closer to me. I don't know if I can absolve him of this. The fact is, Ness is right. I still want to knock the shit out of him for making my mate feel any less than the amazing woman she is, but Shay has a forgiving heart, and as much as I thank the goddess she forgave me, it is hard to reconcile how she can pardon him so easily. Yet I will do as she has asked and give the man a chance. Who knows, there may come a day when I introduce him as my brother and actually mean it. But this is a mammoth... monumental, maybe. We have a long way to go before either of us is ready for this step.

I clear my throat prior to giving her my response. This is equal parts due to Shay and Ness. Just because I found my mate does not mean I will forgo Nessie's safety or happiness, and Brady could represent either of these things.

"I'm learning how to be okay with it because Shay doesn't ask for much, and this is one of the few things she requested. You have to decide if you think his treatment of Shay warrants cutting him off or if his recent steps merit your forgiveness. I will tell you he wasn't as bad to her as the rest."

"Are you running a fever?" she asks with a laugh as she places the back of her hand on my forehead.

"It was damn near impossible to admit, especially out loud."

"I don't know."

"The choice is yours, Ness. Think about what your heart wants and decide if he's worthy of you giving it to him. If so, give the man a chance, and I promise I will too. If not, officially break your bond with him so I don't have to watch you suffer as I did. As I made Shay suffer."

"Fair enough," she replies.

"Good. Because I would hate like hell to have to beat the shit out of him every time he gets near you." Ness's giggles are a sound I love to hear. She continues this until she stands, kisses my cheek, and spins on her heels to leave the room. I don't know if my words will make a lick of difference; I hope they did. Ness deserves the world; I believe he will give it to her. Because if he doesn't, he'll answer to more than just me.

Episode Eighty-Nine: Salt

Brady

AS MUCH AS I detested standing in that office while Foster and Finch judged me, I hated hearing her say she didn't know if she wanted me more. I can understand why she is hesitant. One of the few things she knows about me is I am among the assholes who made Shay's life miserable. Not to mention my dad tried to kill her favorite cousin, and my mom is responsible for collaring Moon.

This punishment was only intended for the worst of the worst within the shifter community. A way to halt a rogue wolf who refuses to listen but does not merit death. From what I am told for your wolf, it is akin to constant shock therapy while your human half feels their pain and hears their cries for help. In my opinion, no wolf deserves this shit. If I had my way, the entire practice would be outlawed. And to know Shay has faced this shit twice confirms how strong she is and what an ignorant asshole I am for not realizing sooner what my mother was capable of.

"Hi, Brady." Then there's Maggie, who is still grieving the loss of Colton. He may not have been her destined mate, but he was her chosen one, and if I hear anyone tell her anything else, they will have to deal with me. I don't care if Foster likes it or not. Colt and Maggie were just as close as any fated mate could be.

"How are you doing today, Maggie?"

"Better." The look I give her confirms I don't believe this. If she were doing better, she wouldn't still be coming to this damn ridge every damn day to look down at his grave.

"Taking everything one day at a time."

"It's the only thing you can do." We sit side by side in silence for the next several minutes. She doesn't have to pretend she is starting to accept his death when she is alone or with me. With me, Maggie doesn't have to hide her heartbreak. She can mourn him how she needs to without fear of what others may think because she knows I am still grieving the loss of my best friend.

"You know, there are times when I feel like he is standing behind me, but when I turn, he's not there. Just empty space."

"It'll take time, Maggie, but I promise you someday it will not be as hard to breathe without him as it is right now."

Tears fill her eyes as she whispers, "I can't sleep unless I hold something of his. Something that smells like him."

"Then don't try."

"Everyone will think I'm weak."

"Then they will have me to contend with because you're one of the strongest people I know."

"If I ask you something, will you tell me the truth?"

"Of course, always." She turns to look at me. Her face displays the pain the question she is desperate to ask is causing. I take her hands in mine, hoping this simple act will comfort her, even if only a little.

"Did Colt really love me? I know you said he did, but did you say that because you thought this was what I needed?"

I'm torn because I don't know if my answer will help or hurt her more. I told her I would always be truthful, but this may be too much for her to handle. So what am I going to do? Lie to her? What kind of an Alpha would I be when I go back on my word at the first chance to prove myself? Hell no. She deserves the truth. We will get through it together once I tell her.

"He was going to ask you to marry him. He had the ring and the place picked out where he wanted to propose. Colt even knew what date he wanted you to become his wife. If you had agreed, he was going to ask if you would consent to the marking ceremony first. He wanted the entire shifter community to know you were his, and he was yours."

Maggie's silent tears turn into a devastating sob, and the sound is the saddest thing I have ever heard. I waste no time pulling her into my arms, hoping to soothe her broken heart. I knew telling her was a risk. Maybe she will be glad to have this information someday, but right now... it's like salt in an open wound.

I can feel her shift seconds before she slips from my grasp to sprint into the woods. I try to follow, but I am unfamiliar with the terrain, and while I am driven by fear of what she may do, she is driven by loss and heartache, making her much faster than Shade and me at the moment.

Racing through the woods, I pray to the goddess for her aid in locating Maggie before anything happens. Mags is not accustomed to these woods, nor is she experienced in traversing the rocky environment. With the rate she is rushing through the trees, she could easily tumble from one of the numerous ledges dotting the mountainside.

No matter how hard I push Shade, I cannot catch up to her, and presently I don't know where I'm at.

Brady, stop forcing me to run around here blindly. I can track her if you give me a damn second to get my bearings.

But we're losing ground.

We will never catch her if you keep making me run around like a damn idiot.

Of course, I know he's right, but my only thought keeps returning to her, lost, alone, and possibly injured. *Colton would never forgive me if something happened to her.*

Well, we aren't doing her any good running in fucking circles, so I'm not asking anymore. I'm taking control.

This is the first time he has ever done something like this, and as hard as I try to retain control, Shade shoves harder to take it until he can finally stop running headlong through the brush.

At first, he stands perfectly still, his ears twitching from one sound to the next until he has the direction he wants to concentrate on. As much as I want to rush off again, he doesn't allow it, opting to lift his nose to scent the air, further narrowing down our path. With this completed, he takes off again, releasing his hold on me.

I was fully prepared to hear his sardonic comments, but thankfully he wanted to find her as badly as I did, which meant he'll hold it until we had her back safe and sound. After that, I will never hear the end of it.

As the trees begin to spread out, becoming less dense, I get the first indication he's on the right track when I see a fresh print in the mud. My heart races when I witness how out-of-control Maggie was as she made her way through here earlier. I know this because the paw prints reveal she was losing traction and sliding more than she was running.

Busting out of the tree line, I discover Maggie, but she's not alone. A man has her pulled against him as she fights to break free. My first instinct is to rush the fucker until I realize he is not trying to hurt her. He's helping her.

My pace slows, and I focus on the tender way he speaks to her. His tone is gentle and calming as he rubs small circles on her back. When I shift and begin to approach, he lifts his hand to wave me off. I notice she is no longer hitting him. Her arms are wrapped around his waist as she cries against his shoulder.

I can't believe he's doing what I couldn't. He's calming her. It's not the fact I discovered someone else here assisting her I find astonishing; it's who the someone else is that I am most amazed by.

Waiting for his eyes to focus back on me, I do the only thing I can. I thank Finch for doing what I couldn't.

Episode Ninety: A Promise

Shay

*T*HIS DAY TOOK one hell of an abrupt turn. It all started with Ness and Brady's revelation and ended with Finch carrying a wrecked Maggie into the pack house. One crazy thing after another, and at this point, I'm waiting for hell to freeze over.

"Hey Shay, Maggie is asking for you," Finch tells me as he leaves her room, closing the door behind him.

Moving towards her room, I hesitate long enough to run my hand down his arm as a show of gratitude for what he did. "Thank you."

"You know me, Shay; I'm a sucker for a damsel in distress."

"Even so, you're a good guy, Finn." I give him a peck on the cheek, which garners the response I figured it would.

"Ah shucks, purdy lady, I'll never wash this cheek again." I roll my eyes at his fake accent.

"Or maybe I'll tease my cousin that his beautiful mate kissed me. He'll love hearing all about it," he tells me with a laugh as he walks towards Foster's office.

I slip into Maggie's room and find her lying on the bed facing the window. The soft sniffles tell me she is still crying. I can't imagine what she's going through. Hell, if something happened to Foster, I don't think I would be as functional as she is.

She waits until I sit next to her on the bed before she whispers her heartbreaking news, and if I didn't already hate Travis and Max, I most assuredly do now. The reality of what they stole from her clenches my heart. She would have had a wonderful life with him. The happiness, the love, the pups, a future, they took it all in one cowardly act.

"Hold on to him, Shay. Hold on to him and never let him go." She doesn't have to elaborate on this. I know she is talking about Foster. Just like I know, she said it because even after everything she's been through, Maggie still has a loving heart, and my friend doesn't want me to ever experience the pain she is feeling.

"I will."

"You have a good life here. If I'm being honest, I didn't understand why you came back with Foster and Finch until recently. It wasn't until we showed up here unwanted—"

"You were never unwanted, Maggie."

"And uninvited—" When I try to interject, she silences me with a look. "but they didn't hesitate. They would have been well within their rights to turn us away; instead, they welcomed us. The entire pack did everything in their power to save the man I…." Her breath hitches as her eyes slip closed. The pained expression settling over her features is hard to see.

She swallows hard, almost like she is trying to push down the sob threatening to overtake her again. Only after Maggie has her emotions under control does she speak again.

"The man I love, which is something I will never be able to repay them for."

There's nothing I can say to dispute this. Maggie's right. After this, we sit in silence, watching the sun drop low in the western sky until a light knock, followed by Ness poking her head in, pulls our focus from the splendor of the day.

"Sorry to interrupt. I wanted to see if you need anything?" Ness has such an enormous heart. She hates to see anyone hurting.

"You're the one who stayed with Colton and took care of him, aren't you?" Maggie asks as she adjusts herself on the bed. Ness, who still blames herself for being unable to save him, drops her head to avoid Maggie's gaze. I know she has wanted to talk to Maggie since Colton died. To tell her how sorry she was that they couldn't save him, but Ness was too ashamed. This is why she went to Whispering Winds, Ash Rock's sister pack, for a while.

She claimed it was to work as their salutary while theirs was away; however, for the people who know her best, we all realized she was having a hard time after losing her first patient.

Foster only agreed to let her go because one of his best friends, Archer, was there to watch over Ness.

Ness takes a deep breath, but I can see the slight tremble of her hand as she gives Maggie the apology she believes she owes her.

"I'm so sorry I couldn't save him. I tried... so damn hard—"

"I know," Maggie tells her. Even with her confirmation, Ness's appearance confirms she doesn't believe this isn't her

Marcelle Valentine

fault. Maggie lifts her hand to Ness, beckoning her to come close, but Ness hesitates. "Please."

This is the last thing Maggie needs to say to get Nessie moving. When Ness places her hand in Maggie's, she is pulled down on the bed so Maggie can hug her.

"Shay told me you never left his side. You were there during his surgery, stayed with him in recovery, and every time I fell asleep, you were there if he needed anything."

"It wasn't enough."

"That's not your fault.... It's not mine, either. I know that now. And I also know Colton wouldn't want us to continue blaming ourselves. So I promise if you help me remember this, I'll help you too."

Ness's eyes finally meet Maggie's, and every emotion she has been holding in spills over as the first tear trickles down her cheek. Both women hold each other as they deal with the loss of Colton.

"I hate to interrupt, but have you decided what to do about Brady, Ness?"

"What about Brady?" Maggie asks as she pulls back, looking from me to Ness.

Ness blows out what I can best describe as an exasperated breath before mumbling, "Well, it seems he's... possibly, although I'm still not sure... I mean, it could have been a mistake."

"Ness." There is no thinking about it; she knows he's her mate.

It's unmistakable when your mate touches you, leaving no room for doubt. It's like a pulse that travels through you, followed by an instant connection. Not just a link. You literally feel pulled to them. Your soul feels whole for the first time as it

32

binds you to your other half. When you find your mate, you feel stronger and healthier. It's like every piece of a puzzle fitting together, and for those who reject it, the bond is never as strong as it would have been with their fated mate.

For the wolves like Foster and me, the ones who try to deny it, the longer you fight it, the more painful it becomes when you're around each other until it either breaks you or you break the bond. By the time Foster and I finally admitted how we felt and were together for the first time, the pain was damn near unbearable.

The only reason Ness didn't realize sooner who Brady was is that when they first arrived, she spent all her time caring for Colton since he was the more critically injured of the two. It was initially touch and go with Brady, but he stabilized fairly quickly. Colt never did. Because of this, her only interaction with Brady was when she would stop in to check on me as I sat vigil over him. But Nessie was never in charge of his care.

It might have been better if she had worked on him because the instant they touched, she would have known, and I'm not sure she would have been able to leave her mate to take care of Colt. This means one of the other salutary would have been assigned to him, and Ness wouldn't be living with the guilt of him dying and her inability to stop it.

She refuses to accept no one could have saved him. No matter how many times any of the others try to convince her.

"He's my mate." I suck in a deep breath, waiting to see how Maggie will react. I shouldn't have said anything. Damn it, I wasn't thinking. Hell, here she is, trying to get over the loss of the man she loves, and I turn around and throw it in her face that Brady found his mate. I'm really a shitty friend.

I hold my breath until she squeals and hugs Ness. "That's fantastic. I'm so happy for Brady and you."

"Umm," Ness's hesitation in Maggie's celebration has Maggie pulling away.

"Am I missing something?"

"I'm unsure if I want Brady to be my mate."

"Why?" Maggie's one-word question is filled with confusion. I'm sure it is partly because, from a young age, every shifter hopes to find their mate. Especially as we enter puberty and gain access to our wolf, this is when we first realize we are missing something. But another part is that she grew up with Brady, and no she-wolf has ever turned down an opportunity to be with him.

Ness's eyes immediately search for mine.

"Oh, I see because of how Shay was treated. You think Brady is an asshole for how she had to grow up."

"I know he is. If I'm being honest, I don't understand how any of you could have treated someone like Shay the way you did... the way you all forced her to live and still be able to look at yourself in the mirror. It's something I'll never understand."

"Ness," I say, trying to diffuse what could quickly become a situation none of us will come back from until Maggie shocks me.

"You're right, and we all know it. At least the ones who have a conscious. None of us will ever be able to justify what we did or forget how we made Shay live, but Brady was trying to improve our pack. He wanted to change things, to make them better. He isn't like his dad or his mom. He's a good man, and if you find it in your heart to look past the mistakes he made as a kid, you may find a man who will prove it to you every day."

Episode Ninety-One: No Secrets

Maximus

TODAY IS A perfect fucking day.

I'm the Alpha of one of the largest packs in the Northwest territory. I took the role by force, which is my favorite way of doing things. My little brother isn't in here whining about when we are going back for the bitch he wants to bed. The ones who oppose me are dead or locked in cages. The recently deceased Alpha's brother is my new ally. Half his sentinels are firmly in my back pocket, along with the former Luna.

A joke of a she-wolf who showed up sniffing around my dick, offering to rule next to me. I fucked her, tossed her clothes at her, and smacked her ass as I sent her scurrying back to the Alpha who wanted her, Sebastian. It seems he coveted something his brother possessed. I don't see the appeal but hey, to each their own. I don't know why the old bitch thought I would claim a washed-up she-wolf. Sadly for her, she was mistaken.

Just like the bitch on her knees under the desk sucking my dick. She may not directly ask, but I know what she wants. Being Luna is a powerful position. Glancing down as she increases the tempo she is working me, I know she has her uses. Luna is not one of them.

"Slow down," I demand as I grip her hair in my fists to guide her the way I want. I don't know what I enjoy watching more... her mouth sliding over the length of my dick or watching her tits bouncing every time I thrust my hips up, forcing her to take me further down her throat.

This chick is nothing more than a she-wolf who thinks she's smarter than she is, but one who knows how to put that trap of hers to good use. I know she doesn't like it when I spill my release in her mouth, but she moans whenever I do, like it's her favorite thing to swallow. Taking every drop like the good little whore she is.

I reach down to grab her breast, rolling her nipple between my fingers. She believes I do this for her pleasure; I don't. I do it for mine. The gasp she gives me every time I apply the right amount of pressure hums along my dick, and it feels good.

"Please fuck me, Max. I'm so horny you have me dripping wet." She pants as she runs her tongue along my shaft.

"Keep doing that. I get off watching you lick my cock," I demand as I squeeze her nipple harder.

The moan she gives me is one I expected, as a trickle of my pre-cum runs down to meet her tongue. She does exactly what I'm waiting for her to do: lick it up before sliding her lips back around me, taking me down to the base as she relaxes her throat the best she can.

I'm close, and as much as I like watching her servicing me, my dick is throbbing to explode my release.

I roughly thrust my hips up again to meet her downward movements while I twist her hair painfully in my grip. My breathing increases as she tries to pull away.

Her hope when I called her here was I planned to fuck her. I won't. Sucking my dick is fine. I reserve fucking it for far better women than her. Like that sweet little piece of ass, my little brother is so desperate to tap.

"Max, we need to talk about our next move," Travis growls as he storms into the office I have claimed as mine. I ignore him, opting to finish what I called her here to do. If he doesn't understand the meaning of a closed door, he can wait until I finish.

He plops in the chair across the desk from me. He knows what I'm doing but doesn't know who I have behind the desk doing it to me.

She tries to pull away, knowing we are no longer alone, but I'm not done, and she will finish what she started. I grab the back of her head and slam myself up three more times before exploding into her mouth.

"Fuck," I yell as I hold her in place, watching her swallow what I generously provide.

I release my grip and rub the back of her head softly, encouraging her to continue licking, which she greedily does as her eyes seek mine, searching them for my approval that she did well. And she did. She always does.

"Ah, fuck. I needed that," I tell her as I slide back to button my pants as she wipes the sides of her mouth. Her eyes widen when she realizes I do not intend to satisfy her needs.

"Wrap this shit up. We have business to deal with," Travis groans as he repositions himself in the chair. He might say this now, but I know he wouldn't object if she wrapped her mouth around his cock instead of mine.

"I'm done. You can come out from under there."

"Are you serious?" she mouths, not wanting Travis to hear who I have in here.

The reason for the little song and dance is she doesn't understand we both know we sometimes fuck the same chicks; she just doesn't know this about us. This dumb she-wolf believes it gives her the upper hand having both brothers.

What she didn't account for is I don't allow secrets. Secrets can crush a growing empire. So, for this reason, Travis and I always get around to telling each other who we are fucking. Even when it's the same bitch.

He simply doesn't know this one has been servicing me for months. He thinks he's the only one she wants, so why should I be the one to dash his fantasy. I said I don't allow secrets, not that I don't have them. Besides, if my brother had asked, I would have told him.

I extend my arms, indicating it's time for her to vacate the seclusion my desk is currently offering.

"I'm not wearing a fucking shirt," she hisses, which I answer with a smirk and a raised eyebrow.

"Erin? You're fucking Erin. When the hell did that start?"

"Well, fucking is a stretch since the only part of her body I've entered is her mouth," I say with a laugh as she climbs out from under my desk with her arms over her chest.

"Shut up, Max," she hisses. But it's hard to take anyone serious when they're yelling at you in nothing but a thong.

"You're fucking my brother?" Travis asks as he glares at her. I may have no issues fucking the same bitch as my brother; sometimes, he does. It seems this may be one of these times.

Erin drops her head, knowing she can't deny it. After all, she's the one who came to me. Not only came to me but came begging me to scratch an itch he doesn't satisfy.

"It seems you aren't enough for this one, little brother."

"What?" He snaps.

"She told me you don't fuck her the way she needs you to. She came to me hoping I would. What was that two months ago, Erin?"

"Travis," she says, reaching for her shirt, but Travis interrupts her by grabbing her wrist and pulling her onto his lap.

"Since then, she's had my cock in her mouth as often as you've had your dick inside the pussy she keeps begging me to fill."

"I'm not enough for you, huh? Do you need my brother's cock too? Is that it, Erin? You want both brothers?" He asks her as he grinds her hips over his groin.

He keeps this up until he has her worked up enough she no longer cares he caught her with my dick in her mouth.

"Can we go back to your room?" Her question comes out more as a pant than a request. She wants to be fucked, and right now, she doesn't care which of us does it. She wants to come. Can't blame her for that.

"You didn't care to be in Max's room, so you can keep grinding on my dick right here," he murmurs in her ear. When she attempts to spin to face him, he stops her.

"No. You think I want the mouth filled with my brother's come anywhere around my face."

"Travis, I'm sorry." Her apology is admirable, if not complete bullshit, since her fingers are playing with her nipples, and she's looking at the wrong brother.

Marcelle Valentine

"I'm not. Now shut up and ride my cock or suck it. Your choice." This silences any further objections as he increases her moving hips.

"We need to come up with a game plan, Max," he groans, pulling her down harder. Her breathing increases as her eyes focus on me. Is she fantasizing it's my cock she is grinding against? I think she is. Dirty little girl.

Tilting my head to the side, I watch my brother work to bring her to the edge before stopping to let her crash back down without the sweet release of the orgasm she desperately seeks. My dick twitches as I watch her lick her lips, knowing she still tastes me on them.

"You want to collect your trophy that bad, little brother?"

"Damn straight I do," he tells me as his hands slide up her sides to find her waiting breast. He no longer has to move her hips. Erin is frantically doing this for him. I wonder if she would be riding him like she is if she knew the trophy we are talking about is a sexy little blonde named Shay.

He must be done playing with her since Trav lifts her ass to release his cock before he slams her down on him, burying himself deep inside her.

There was nothing gentle about the way he handled her. That's not my brother's way, but it doesn't seem to bother this one. She likes it like this. The rougher he is with her, the wetter she gets. The moan she releases confirms she likes him fucking her right here as much as she wants me to watch.

"Am I fucking you the way you want now," he growls as he yanks her hair to pull her ear next to his mouth.

"Yes," she cries out.

"You get off having someone watch my cock screwing this wet pussy, don't you?"

40

"Yes."

"Is that what you want, an audience? Maybe next time I can fuck you while the entire pack watches us."

"Oh, goddess," she cries as her fingers twist her nipples.

"Dirty fucking bitch. Tell me how wet you are."

"I'm soaked."

"You're dripping all over my cock." He bites her ear hard enough he draws blood.

"Yes."

"You want me to keep fucking you until you come, Erin?"

"Don't stop, please."

As if he doesn't have a woman riding his dick ready to come, he looks back at me to finish what he came in to say.

"We need to leave soon. I don't know how long I can wait," Travis tells me as I move to the front of my desk to lean against it. I don't miss her eyes dropping to the erection, growing harder as I watch her tits bouncing every time he drills into her.

"I have some recon coming my way. As soon as we have it, we'll go."

"Promise?" He pants as he bites into her shoulder.

"Yep."

"Good. I'll finally claim what should have always been mine."

"I guess you will."

"Oh, goddess, I'm going to come," Erin cries as she reaches behind her to pull Travis back to the spot he was biting seconds ago. But instead of letting her find her release, he holds her steady against him as he leans up, pressing his mouth against her ear.

"You like having my brother's cock in your mouth?" Erin's eyes moved from mine to look over her shoulder at Travis for the first time since he grabbed her. "I asked you a question?"

"Yes," she whispers as her eyes shoot back over to me. The grin I give her has her licking her lips again.

"Stand up and lean forward," he directs as he keeps himself seated inside her. She obediently obeys. He only moves again when she is positioned in front of me, hands on my thighs to brace herself from the punishing rhythm my brother has already returned to.

"Well, what are you waiting for, Erin?" He asks, slowing his hips from the back-and-forth motion she is begging for as his hands wrap around to find her clit.

"What?"

"My brother's waiting." She takes a second to look up at me. The only response she receives is my eyebrows raising. This is all the confirmation she needs as she pops the button on my jeans to get to one of her new favorite playthings.

My hands find her nipples rock hard and begging to be played with.

"Or is this how you want to be fucked? With me filling your pussy while my brother fills your mouth?" His hand works faster, rubbing her clit until she moans loud enough for the entire pack house to know she is being fucked in here.

"Then we'll fuck you like the whore you are." Apparently, being called a whore isn't a turnoff for this chick. Quite the opposite. Her moans grow louder as she greedily takes me into her mouth again while Travis rams into her from behind.

Episode Ninety-Two: Petition

Riona

MY SMILE COULDN'T get any sweeter as I look across the desk at my last hope of getting close to Foster.

"Yes, sir. I just moved here."

"And you know about the pack how?"

"My uncle. I believe you know him. Seamus?"

"Seamus is your uncle? Well, I'll be. It's a small world, isn't it?"

"It would seem so," I tell him with enough sugary sweetness to keep a dentist in business for years. The smile he gives me tells me everything I need to know. He's hooked.

I had little doubt when I found out about this one; I had my way in. Thank goddess, he seems more intent on keeping his eyes off my tits than using care to ask me the key questions he should have. Like, why did you leave your last pack? What brought you to the states? Do you know any of our pack members? Would any of them be willing to vouch for you? What benefit can you bring to our pack?

Let's be honest; unless I want this old wolf to blush, keeping the benefits I offer between the Alpha and I would be best.

And the most important question of all…. Do you believe our Alpha will welcome you into our family? I think it's fairly easy to guess the answer to this particular question. Although if I gain access to this pack, my priority will be to change his mind and do it in the most delicious way.

"I'm sure our Alpha won't have an issue approving this, especially after he finds out who your uncle is."

"Truly," I say as I lean forward, giving him a clear view of the breast I refuse to restrain with a bra. The shirt I chose is a loose off-the-shoulder little sweater, and leaning forward across the desk as I am, the second he looks up, he is staring directly at the unrestrained tits he has tried to avoid looking at the entire time we've been in here.

His eyes shoot to mine after taking a few seconds to admire my assets. It's cute how uncomfortable I've made him, as apparent by his repeated attempts to clear his throat.

"I'll put the petition on his desk myself."

"Thank you," I squeal as I rush around, hug him, and bounce from my perceived excitement. What I'm actually doing is giving this old dog a thrill. I'll make sure he fights for me to join, as I will with every other male in this pack.

"You're welcome," he tells me. After a second, he pulls my arms from behind his neck before patting my hand. To late beta, I already felt the effect I had over you.

"Ian, you are a wonderful man. I won't forget what you've done for me."

"No thanks necessary. Seamus may not be a shifter, but he's as much a part of our pack as anyone else, and his family members are always welcome."

"He is a wonderful man. Without him, I would have never found this quaint little town or your wonderful pack. You don't know how happy you've made me."

"Well, we'll have to remember to thank him as well. In the meantime, would you like a tour of our community?"

"Doesn't the Alpha have to approve this?" I ask, tapping the paper he filled out on me. "Before I am permitted to wander around here?"

"It's only a formality with your references. You're guaranteed to be granted a place in our pack. But you are correct. Someone will have to escort you until Foster approves." He picks up the phone, asking someone named Danny to come to his office.

What a sweet little name. A cute nickname for the man or boy I plan to wrap around my slender fingers.

"I have a few things to work out with my family, so you may not see me around a lot for a couple of weeks, but I want you to know how grateful I am for this opportunity."

"Is everything okay with Seamus?"

"Oh, yeah, Uncle Seamus is fine. My mom is ill and back in Ireland by herself. I may have to fly back for a week or two to help get everything squared away."

"I'm sorry to hear about your mom."

"Thanks. She's moving in with my sister, but they wanted to renovate before she does, so if it's not finished, I'm going back home to stay until Narissa can come to get her."

"Well, that's sweet of you." Or the opportunity I need to move around pack land as much or as little as I want with no

45

interference since you won't expect to see me. It also gives me the excuse not to formally align with the pack because I plan to do it as their Luna when I do. Not as some random ass she-wolf.

"Family is everything. Right?"

"That they are." As if on cue, my escort arrives. A young wolf who can't be much older than eighteen, nineteen at the most.

While he isn't much younger than me, the wide-eyed innocent look he gives me confirms I will have no issues controlling him and our movement around pack lands today.

"Danny, this is Riona. Riona, Danny. You'll be showing Riona around today."

"Happy to help, Beta," he responds, as any good wolf would. But this is where his manners end because the second Ian turns his back, Danny's eyes flick down to the boobs I imagine he's hoping to see today.

Cute.

Never going to happen, but cute.

When he looks back up, he realizes I caught him checking me out, and the grin I give him has him standing a little taller.

"Seamus is Riona's uncle." His shoulders tighten as he figures out I'm not just some random she-wolf. Seamus seems to have a fair amount of pull in this pack. I like it. Maybe after I'm Luna, I'll bring him further into the fold. Maybe. This all depends on how well he accepts things around Lake and this pack under my rule.

"Well, thanks again, Ian," I say as I give him a quick peck on the cheek. Danny's watchful eyes are observing our every interaction. Hmmm. I can use this. Danny patiently waits for me to exit the room.

As we walk through their pack lands, I notice his hand has found its way to my lower back more times than I can count.

He shows me all the normal stuff. A pack house. The medical center. The fighting arena. Their training quarters. And, of course, he avoids everything I want to see. The Alpha's office, his personal quarters... his bed.

"So I haven't had the pleasure of meeting your Alpha today."

"I think he took off this morning with his cousins, a couple newer pack members, and his girlfriend." I have to restrain myself from growling when he refers to this pathetic bitch as his girlfriend.

Not wanting to seem overly eager regarding his whereabouts, I seethe in silence as I refrain from asking further questions. I need someone to help me work off all this negative energy, and I know the perfect specimen. A tall, hot as fuck, strong biker with a chip on his shoulder regarding yours truly.

It doesn't take Danny long before our tour takes us away from the main pack territory and into a more secluded area.

"So one place my old pack always showed new recruits was the Alpha's house. Did we see your Alpha's place today?" I saw a large home, and I suppose this could pass as a house worthy of a normal Alpha and Luna, but it won't suit the needs of Foster and me after we are mated.

"Foster's place isn't inside the main area, but he has a suite in the pack house he stays at from time to time."

"That's not normal for the Alpha to live away from his pack."

"Foster never wanted to be the Alpha. He bought his cabin before taking the role and doesn't want to let it go. Besides, I think Shay likes his cottage." Of course, someone like her would like to live at the ass end of nowhere.

Oh, I don't plan on making him get rid of the cottage. It can be our fuck house when I want things a little more adventurous than pack life allows. But let me make this clear we *Will Not* live there.

"Foster tried to give the Alpha house to Ian to tempt him to stay on as his beta, but Ian refused."

"Ian isn't your beta?"

"Yeah, he is for now. Until Foster finds someone to take his position. And trust me, he isn't too worried about finding someone to fill the role," Danny tells me with a laugh.

"Oh, good. I thought maybe I had spoken to the wrong person."

"Nope, Ian's the man you wanted." Oh, sweet, talkative Danny, Ian is most certainly not the man I want.

Hoping to keep this nitwit talking, I put my foot up on a low stump and bend over to retie a shoe that doesn't need the attention I'm giving it.

"Is his home far from here?" Danny turns around to find my boobs on display for his viewing pleasure. He shifts slightly, and I listen to him as he forces himself to swallow.

"Yeah."

"Where is it?"

"Southwestern corner of our pack lands," he mumbles. Switching to the other shoe, I continue pretending I'm oblivious to where his eyes are focused.

"All by himself?"

"Yeah," he stammers as he steps closer.

"And he stays there most of the time?"

"Anytime Shay isn't coming over after work and any night she doesn't work. Unless he stays at Shay's house."

"How often is he out there all alone?"

"A few times a week." It's like my tits have him mesmerized. Magical tits. Yet another thing I can add to my resume. Granted,

I'm sure I wouldn't have this level of control if the man was older, wiser, and had gotten his dick wet more than a handful of times. It seems luck is on my side today.

"Do you know when he'll be out there alone again?"

"Dunno. Is there a reason you're so interested in the Alpha?" Oops, one question too many. Looking up, I find his eyes still taking in the sway of my breast.

"Ahem, my eyes are up here, sport." His eyes snap to mine as his arms come around to cover the erection he is donning.

"I should probably get you back before it gets dark."

"Uh-huh." I notice how closely he follows behind me and how fast he reaches to pull me back from any exposed root that he informs me I almost tripped over. It's ironic how often his crotch is pressed against my ass on our return trip. I let it go. I figure it's the least I can do for all the helpful information he provided me today.

By the time we return to the pack house, the day has slipped away to evening, and as much as he thought he was going to escort me to my uncle's car. He's mistaken. I have one last task I need to complete before I leave.

"Can I use the restroom before I go?"

"Sure, do you need me to—"

"I think I can manage." For this, I don't need an audience.

Episode Ninety-Three: Flyboy

Foster

TODAY WENT BETTER than I figured it would. It was Shay's idea. She thought we needed to get away from pack land and spend time with our friends. I recommended skiing. She wanted something warmer.

When I laughed, she understood why being in the cold would appeal to me. I can't help it. My mate makes it hard on me not to keep her in bed all day. Especially when she moans my name the way she does. It's one of the sweetest damn sounds I have ever heard.

But in the end, she got what she wanted. Was there any doubt I would cave to her every desire?

The best part was seeing Maggie smile for the first time since Colton died. I think she was laughing more at Brady, who tripped over himself every time Ness was near, than smiling because she is happy, but I count it as a win either way.

She's a sweet woman who's been through enough lately. I'm most amazed by the relationship between her and Finch. It's not romantic. It's one lost soul leaning on another in their time of need, and I've never witnessed Finn more attentive than when he's tending to her. In the truest sense of the word, she needs friendship now more than anything else. Safety and security without expectations, and he more than gives this to her.

While Finn and I toss the football around, Brady does what any man trying to prove himself would do: cleaning and packing the truck for our ride home so Ness doesn't have to do any of it.

When Ness trips and Brady catches her, I don't miss how long she stays wrapped in his arms until she shakes him off. Leaving him standing there with his hands clasped behind his head, looking at the sky. She walks over to where I'm standing when she sees me laughing at him after their interaction.

"Ness, when are you going to put this man out of his misery?"

"I'm not done making him grovel yet."

"Wait. You already know you aren't going to break your mate bond, and you haven't told him?"

"Yes and No."

"You wanna tell me why?"

"Because I'm not done torturing him for how he treated Shay."

"Ness," I say, tilting my head.

"Don't you Ness me, Foster."

"You know Shay wouldn't want you to do that. Right?"

"That's why I didn't tell her, and neither will you. This is my punishment for Brady, not hers. If he wants to be with me, then he has to prove he's worth my time."

"While I agree with the last part, you can't use Shay as your reason."

"I can because I am, and you can't stop me."

"First of all, little cousin, I can stop it. Furthermore, Shay would hate it—"

"So don't tell her," she interrupts.

"And... I won't lie to her," I finish.

"I didn't tell you to lie. I'm telling you to keep your mouth shut."

"Vanessa, I'm not seeing the distinction," I say, turning away from my game with Finn.

"Cousin pact."

Damn it! The one thing she could say to guarantee my silence. It was a promise the three of us made as kids that when one of us said this, the others couldn't tell anyone else. There were only two stipulations. It couldn't be dangerous, and the three of us were exempt from the pact. Meaning we could tell each other, but no one else. In all rights, most sane people would consider it dangerous... especially since this means I'll be keeping her secret from my mate. A mate who doesn't like secrets.

"This is going to blow up in your face and mine too, apparently."

"Doesn't matter. Cousin pact," she says as she strolls back over to where Shay and Maggie are collecting the rest of our stuff.

"Oh shit, Nessie invoked the pact. Do tell?" Finn asks as he jogs over to where I'm still holding the football.

"It seems our little terrorist knows she isn't going to break her bond with Brady, but she's making him sweat as payback for how Shay was treated."

"And Shay's okay with it?"

"She doesn't know."

"Damn, cuz, you're so screwed if Shay finds out," he says with a laugh as he knocks the ball from my hand and jogs over to where the rest of them are waiting.

"Tell me about it," I say to the empty space around me.

****

We arrive back at Lake with barely enough time to drop Shay off at work. After walking her inside, I kissed her before telling her I would be back as soon as I could.

She knows she is not to leave this bar without either Finch, Brady, Atlas, Denver, or me. I realize this might be overkill; my beautiful mate repeatedly tells me as much, but I don't care. I won't take any chances as long as those assholes are still out there.

I wouldn't have left her here if I hadn't signed up for patrol duty tonight to show Brady the ropes. But I need to do this. I wish Shay had told Seamus no when he asked her to fill in for Mandy. The only reason I agree to this shit situation is Finn told me he would hang out at the bar. On my tab, of course.

It's a small price to pay for her safety.

"You know we don't have to do this tonight. I'm sure I can talk one of the other sentinels into taking me out to show me around the territories."

"No, it's fine. I can't shake off the feeling...."

"What?" Brady asks as he looks around the bar.

Marcelle Valentine

"Nothing. Let's go. The sooner we start, the sooner I can get back here."

Rather than driving back to pack land, we can shift in the woods behind Stooges and start our patrol from here. Besides, seeing my truck out here may lead others to believe I'm inside.

Shadow perks up within seconds of shifting, and I notice Brady's wolf Shade is focused on mine.

Brother? Shadow questions.

Brother. Shade confirms as they move next to one another.

I can't believe how quickly they recognized each other. Or how fast they seem to bond as they race each other through the night. They never met each other, yet they accepted the other as a part of themselves. Something Brady and I are moving towards, but we haven't made it there yet. I guess we could each take a lesson from our other half. The one thing I realize that differs from any other wolf is that even though Brady hasn't officially joined my pack, I can mind-link with him since we're siblings.

This makes our travels and the patrol move along faster than I anticipated. When I realize how close we are to Atlas and Denver's bar, I stop there to introduce Brady to Madge. A long time ago, Atlas made a spot for Finn and me to hide clothes for times like this. When we find ourselves at their end of town and want to stop by for a drink. Besides, we have a standing invitation anytime we want to go there.

Shifting back, I pass some of my clothes over to Brady. I'm taller and bulkier than my brother, but my clothes still fit him better than Finn's would.

"Where are we?"

"This is Atlas and Denver's place."

"I'm not so sure Atlas is my biggest fan. I did try to beat his ass."

"Try is the optimal word here, Brady," I tell him with a laugh as I push the buzzer next to the door.

"Still, are you sure he'll be okay with me in his place?"

"Atlas doesn't hold grudges. Besides, he knows why you did it, and he would have done the same."

"What, get his ass kicked?"

"I'm not sure any of us could beat his ass."

"Damn. I'm glad to hear that." I laugh as I clap him on the back before leading him inside.

After making a few quick introductions, I excuse myself to Madge's back office to call Finn and check on how things are going. It seems all the nervous energy was for nothing since everything is fine. Not only is it good, but it's also great since Ness met up with her friends at the bar. And somehow talked Maggie and Sadie into joining her.

For the first time since leaving her, I relax enough to enjoy a few drinks with my friends. After an hour and several drinks later, Brady must be feeling good because he asked me something I never expected.

"How the hell did you manage to hold Shay at arm's length for so long?"

"Why do you want to know?" I cautiously ask him. I'm unsure where this is going. But I can tell you one thing: if Shay's love life is the direction the conversation is heading, I don't want to talk about it with the man who, not so long ago, wished to take my mate from me. On the flip side, if he wants to talk about Ness and him, I'm also not so sure I want to go there either since I still see my cousin as the sweet little kid who followed Finn and me around when we got in trouble.

"Well, Ness. She won't talk to me, and I don't want to push her, but she makes it so damn hard when she looks so fucking—"

"Hey-hey-hey. That's still my little cousin you're talking about."

"I can assure you Ness is all woman, Foss," Denver informs me, and the growl I give him is only outdone by the one rumbling out of the man next to me.

"It seems someone has it bad for our sweet little Ness," Denver says, ruffling Brady's hair. I have little doubt if Denver wasn't the size of a barn, Brady wouldn't have let him get away with this shit.

"Something like that," Brady grumbles as he combs his fingers through the mess left by Denver.

"It would seem our sweet little Ness found her mate," I correct as I take a sip of the scotch Madge poured for us.

Denver looks from me to Brady. He's a great guy but not as quick on the uptake, so the three of us sit here waiting for him to catch up with what the rest of us already know. I know he's finally put it together when his eyes turn into silver dollars.

"Oh, shit. Foster means you. You're Nessie's mate. Damn. Home fucking run, brother. Nessie is a fine ass catch." Again, a low growl reverberates through Brady.

"I'm going to laugh when Foster or his brother here beats your ass," Atlas tells him as he nods for Madge to bring over another round.

"Let Ness hear you call her that asshole, and you won't have to worry about my brother or me beating your ass; she'll do it herself."

"Why? I call her Nessie all the time," Brady says as he looks from Atlas to me.

"And she hears you say it?"

"Yeah, I call her Nessie almost every time we talk."

"Because, oh clueless brother of mine, my cousin equates this name to the Loch Ness monster. You know, the one they call Nessie."

"Oh…. Fuck."

"Yeah."

"Why the hell didn't she say anything? I would never have kept calling her this if I knew. Shit, she hates me because there's no other reason to explain why she didn't say anything."

"Cause she wants your sweet, sweet lovin'." Denver doesn't wait for our growl this time as he slams the shot Madge sat down in front of us.

"Keep it up, flyboy," I tell him with just enough malice to make my frustration sound real.

"Don't listen to these chuckleheads," Madge interjects as she takes a shot with us. "If a girl lets you get away with something she doesn't let anyone else do, it's normally because she likes you more than the chuckleheads surrounding you."

"Madge, are you calling me a chucklehead?" I ask, feigning heartbreak.

"Only cause you're acting like one. Now stop giving this one a hard time," Madge tells me as she tosses her towel at us before walking to the other end of the bar.

"Yes, ma'am."

"Getting better, Foster," Madge yells from the other end of the bar.

After we finish the next round, we say our goodbyes because I'm eager to see my mate, and Brady seems almost as antsy to get back when he hears Ness is at Stooges.

Marcelle Valentine

"Do you think she's right? You know about Nessi—" he stops himself before he can finish the name she hates. "Ness?"

"I can tell you she's never let anyone else call her that before you." We remain silent as we remove the clothes and drop them into the chute Atlas had put in for us to place the clothes we had on while we were here. I think Madge washes them and returns them to our hiding spot. I told her once she didn't have to do it, but the only response I got was it must have been fairies.

"Hey, why did you call Denver flyboy?"

"That's not my tale to tell," I advise as we shift into our wolves and race back to the women we are both desperate to see.

Episode Ninety-Four: About Time

Shay

$\mathcal{H}$YDE LAUGHS AT me again when I try to hide another yawn. I'm exhausted, and as enjoyable as today has been, I'll be glad when my shift ends. My bed is not only calling my name... it's screaming it.

I had to work later than planned last night when Mandy screwed me over and pretended she was sick. It was utter bullshit, and if I were saying it out loud, air quotes would have been involved. She wasn't ill; she just hasn't gotten over the fact Foster wants me and not her. Hell, one of her best friends who was here last night repeated the sentiment several times.

I also had to get up early today to prepare everything for the picnic I talked Foster into having. Since it was my idea, not his, it was only fair that I take on the bulk of the preparation.

One would think the picnic today would be all about kicking my feet up, resting, eating, and soaking up the sun, but nope. Instead, I had to play the part of a counselor for Ness so she could bitch about Brady. I don't know why this girl won't admit she likes him, especially since she spent as much time accidentally—on purpose—bumping into him as she did bitching about him following her around like a lost puppy. Her words, not mine.

"You gonna make it there, kiddo?" Hyde asks, handing me the money to pay for his beer.

"Damn, I hope so. I don't imagine Seamus would be thrilled with me if he walked out and found me sleeping on the bar."

"You just," as you can imagine, he hiccups here, "climb up here and have a little ol' fiesta," Jerry slurs as he taps the bar.

"Siesta," I correct him cause I am sure as shit not planning a party.

"That's what I said," he confirms as he tries to widen his eyes before he covers one of them, mumbling, "there you are."

"Jer, are you alright over there?"

"Like a fine wine, pickled, corked," hiccup, "and age to perfection." He kisses his fingers and opens them like a chef who created a masterpiece.

Mandy slams through the door with the same chick who gave me a hard time last night. Great. Just fan-fuckin-tastic. This is the last thing I need; the only thing that could make this any better would be if Riona shows up. I mean, then it would be a party. The Foster-loving fan club party.

"Hey you, how about you stop gawking and start serving," the girl with Mandy says as she snaps her fingers at me. Mandy slides out of her coat as her eyes surf around the bar. One guess who she's looking for.

"I mean fuck, I know we are goddamn hot, but really not interested in you. But that desirable piece of ass, Foster—"

Ness shifts enough in her chair to gain a clearer view of the chick, giving me a hard time, but when Mandy interjects, I don't miss the faint growl coming from her.

"Nora, he's mine. Get your own hot piece of ass." Even though Foster has never given me any reason to doubt him, Mandy and Riona are beautiful women, and I can't help but wonder if they push hard enough if he would change his mind.

"I think you know better than that, Mandy," Hyde mumbles before he takes a drink from his beer.

"Oh, Hyde, give it up. It's probably never going to happen," she says, her eyes meeting mine before she corrects herself with a snarl, "or maybe it will."

"What the hell are you talking about, Mandy?" Hyde snaps as he slams his beer down harder than he should have. The force causes the beer to foam inside the bottle and spill over on his hand.

"Everyone knows you want a certain blonde who doesn't know her place." Nora's gaze burns into me, and her smirk causes me to roll my eyes.

"What can I get you two?" I snap, trying to keep the anger under control, but the fury wins out, and it leeches out in my response.

Ness strolls up to the bar with Sadie close behind. Her drink is full, so I can only assume she's here for moral support. She claims the stool beside Jerry, and he gives her a beaming smile.

"I'll take a Pop My Cherry," Nora says as she looks over at Finn, who's completely unaware of her sexual advances since he's busy leaning back in his chair chatting with some of the guys from the mill.

"Too late," Ness mumbles, and I have to stifle a laugh.

"Did you say something?" Nora asks Ness, but she doesn't respond; instead, the only answer this girl will get is a nasty glare.

Mandy, who still hopes to win Foster, understands that pissing off his favorite cousin isn't the way to do it. She quickly switches from the barely restrained loathing tone I got to a sickly sweet one.

"Ness, oh my god, I didn't know you were coming in tonight. Nora, this is Ness, Foster's cousin. Ness, this is—"

"Nora. Yeah, I got that."

"So tell us where your sexy cousin is tonight?" Nora asks as she looks at me.

"Sadie, this is Mandy and, apparently, Nora. Mandy thinks she stands a snowball's chance in hell of winning over Foster. It seems she is just as delusional as that cow Riona is." Ness's focus slowly shifts from Sadie to the two women sitting there with their mouths gaped open. Sadie must want to get in on the action because she peers around Ness, laughing a little.

Five minutes later, both women have their drinks. Ness and Sadie are back to ignoring them as Mandy and Nora whisper to one another. Too bad for them, we can hear every word they are saying, and I swear to the moon goddess, if she makes one more comment about the size of Foster's dick, I'm going to knock a bitch out.

When the door flies open this time, I'm shocked to see Brady strolling through it. I figured they would be on patrol for several more hours.

"Well, he can fuck me anytime," Nora mutters. After weeks of Ness's indecision, something shifts as a menacing growl rumbles through her. Before Nora can say anything else, Ness stalks over to Brady and kisses him.

Yeah, I remember that. Of course, when I did it to Foster, we were involved. Poor Brady had no clue it was coming. She actually stunned him, but it only took a second for him to recover. His arms are around her in a flash to hold her in place, prolonging what she started.

"About damn time," Maggie yells while Finn shakes his head.

Episode Ninety-Five: Man of My Word.

Foster

WALKING INTO THE bar, I admit being shocked when I find Ness in Brady's arms with her mouth smashed against his. It doesn't take me long to figure out what happened. Mandy's here, and the chick she has with her glares at Nessie like she just took her favorite toy.

I know this couldn't be further from the truth. Since the day Brady discovered Ness was his mate, he has only had eyes for my sweet little cousin.

"Hey beautiful," I say, strolling up to the bar to greet the woman I only have eyes for.

"Hi, Foss. I didn't expect to see you so soon."

"We may have had an incentive to wrap things up quick," I tell her as I pick her hand up to kiss it, which earns me a smile from Shay.

"You better get Brady before this evening takes an X-rated turn."

"I don't know; it looks like something I might enjoy."

"Kissing Ness?" She asks with a little laugh, but when I lean over to give her my response, I replace the teasing merriment with a blush.

"Keep it up, beautiful, and you will swiftly find yourself over my knee while I whip that sweet little ass of yours. Let's see if we can make your backside as rosy as your cheeks." Her mouth falls open, but it only takes her a second before her teeth rake over her lower lip. It seems my little mate might enjoy it. At the very least, she's definitely contemplating it.

Leaning further into her personal space, I put my lips against her ear to whisper, "If you keep looking at me like that, I'm going to take you right here, right now."

Her forced swallow as her eyes shift around the bar has me laughing this time. Before I pull away, I run my tongue over the spot on her neck I plan to mark soon, and the shiver it produces has me wishing we were any place but here.

"Get a damn room, you two," Finn yells from the table behind me. When I turn to tell him to shut up, I realize he isn't talking to me. Brady is making up for lost time with Ness since he has her against the wall, and her legs are wrapped around his waist.

With my attention diverted from her, Shay takes this opportunity to step out of my reach. Even in the low light, I can see her breathing has increased and a faint shimmering glow in her eyes as Moon responds to Shadow's growl of dominance.

Yeah, we will need to have that marking conversation soon because every time I am with her, Shadow pushes me to claim our mate, and before long, I will not be able to resist his demands.

I can tell you one thing when I claim her, and she claims me... it won't be in the middle of Stooges and certainly won't be in front of an audience. So I decide it is past time to join Finch, Maggie, and Sadie before I do something I might regret.

"Hi, Foster," Mandy's tone conveys her frustration that she is not the woman I want.

"Hey." This is all she will get from me. I know how she treats Shay, and I don't fucking like it.

Half an hour later, I am counting the seconds until this place closes, and I can take my mate home and ravage every part of her. My dick is hard just thinking about her writhing under me as I make her scream my name. Watching her ass shake as she wipes down the bar has me vacating my chair, so I can tell her what I plan to do.

If I have to sport this fucking hard-on for another two hours, then I want to know her pussy is wet and throbbing with need.

The moon goddess must be smiling at me today because she bends over to pick up a discarded napkin just as I arrive behind her. Pulling her back against the fucking erection, desperate to be free of these jeans, her gasp as she feels me against her has my cock jumping with anticipation.

"Can you leave soon?" I breathe as my hands slide down her side.

"Um... well... I don't...." Good, I have her almost as flustered as I am. A low growl reverberates through my chest when my hands drop to her hips.

"Is everything okay?" Her wary eyes inform me she does not yet know what I discovered.

I pull her ass more firmly against the stiff erection, growing harder by the second. "What did I tell you?"

When she looks over her shoulder again, the question I find in her eyes remains.

"What do you have on?"

"What?" she asks as she tries to fully turn to look at me; however, I want her right where she is. My fingers tap her hips, making her gasp when she realizes what I have already figured out.

"What did I tell you I would do to you if I found you wearing these?"

"Oh, fuck," she mumbles as she fully realizes what I am talking about.

"Exactly right." And fucked, she shall soon be.

"Seriously, Foster."

"What. Did. I. Tell. You?"

"I'm at work," she hisses as my fingers continue to tap the panties I know I will find when I take off her pants.

"You didn't answer my question."

"You'd take them off me." While throaty with her need, her rushed response tells me she fears I will uphold this promise. And I will. I am a man of my word, and the thought of seeing her stripped bare in front of me has my dick thick and humming from the mere vision.

My hand wraps around to pop the button of her jeans as I bury my face in her hair.

"Foster, there are people in here. And I know you won't remove my clothes and expose me to everyone." Is this a taunt? A dare? Or does my mate need me to prove how much control I possess in this town?

Marcelle Valentine

"Get out. Everyone!" I growl as I pop the button, and the gasp she gives me causes a snarl from Shadow and me when these assholes don't move fast enough.

"Foster, Seamus is going to fire me."

"I said get the fuck out of here." I pull the zipper one tooth at a time, and everyone, aside from two exceptions, is up and moving toward the door. Mandy and her fucking friend Nora.

"I'm not done yet," Nora snaps, which causes my eyes to shoot over to her. Shadow pushes forward, and the growl I give this time has both of them scampering out of the fucking bar.

When the door slams shut, I yank her pants down as my lips come to her neck, and the moan she grants us breaks the last bit of my resolve.

Episode Ninety-Six: Fulfilling a Promise

Shay

I GUESS THIS teaches me not to doubt him. I admit it surprised me when everyone got up to leave the bar, but I was damn astonished when I watched Seamus going with them. It's his business after all, but he submitted to Foster like any member of the Ash Rock pack would, even though he's not.

At first, I want to tell him we can't do this here, but his lips on my neck as his hands dip into my panties erase any thought of telling him to wait.

"I'm glad you made the conscious choice to test me on this," he murmurs in my ear. The heat from his breath tickles my neck and pebbles my nipples.

His hands on my hips force me to turn so he can look at me as he slides my pants down and discards them without a second thought. With the object that started this interaction on full

Marcelle Valentine

display, he takes a step back. His hazel eyes slide down my body, taking in the lacey little thong I made the mistake of putting on this morning. As exposed as I feel standing in the middle of Seamus's bar, I am equally aroused.

His hand comes up and circles, suggesting he wants me to spin for him. I comply because I want him to look as much as he wants to see.

When I have my back to him, I stop to chance a glance over my shoulder, and what I find has my pussy throbbing with anticipation as I wait with bated breath for him to tell me what to do next.

"That fucking sexy little ass of yours will look even better when it's wrapped around my cock, Shay." A shiver runs up my back as I contemplate his words. Did he mean like in general? He surely isn't implying *that*, or does he intend to do what he said?

My pulse quickens as thoughts of him taking me from behind play out in my head, and I can feel the heat traveling from my head to my toes. It's like a jolt of electricity that flows straight to my core.

"Turn, Shay, or I'm going to bend you over right now and punish that ass before I get to enjoy you the way I want." I suck in a breath, realizing he intends to punish my backside as he has done to the place now pulsing with need. If he doesn't touch me soon, I think I might burst.

"Drop your shirt." I comply.

"Your bra too. Let me see if those nipples are ready for my tongue." If they weren't already rock hard, they would have pebbled the instant he told me this. I don't miss how lopsided this is. I'm standing before him in nothing but a thong while Foster remains completely dressed.

"Take off the thong and hand it to me." I hesitate since I know nothing will stop him from taking me in the middle of my boss's establishment once I do this.

"I want you to give me the thing you should never have put on today, beautiful." Sliding my fingers around the tiny scrap of material, I exhale as I remove the lace wet from my excitement.

I can't stop the moan rushing out of me as I watch him lift them to his nose and inhale the musk of my arousal before he places them in his back pocket. I wonder where in the hell he keeps putting the panties he takes from me because he doesn't return them.

Before I can move, he's on me, placing me on top of the bar. The triumphant smirk he gives tells me he likes this little game he created.

His hands slide up my thighs before he spreads my legs so he can see how his words and actions affect me. If the dampness coating my legs is anything to go by, I can tell you he will find me dripping wet and ready for him to fill me.

"I did warn you."

"Foster." He silences any further protest when he runs his finger along the slit of my pussy, and I jump from the contact.

"So fucking wet for me already," he growls before burying a finger, followed by a second deep inside me while he pulls his shirt, popping one button after another. "I'm going to lick this pussy until you scream my name."

My fingers knot in his hair as I try to pull his face to my throbbing clit. I nearly jump off the bar from the contact when he finally brings his mouth down against me. His tongue sweeps along one side, followed by the other, and I know it will not take long.

His dominance over me and the entire bar was a huge turn-on. I like him controlling me. I like his alpha male attitude, and as gentle as he is with me any other time, I love it when he is rough and demanding when he fucks me.

My body is ready to let loose, prepared to submit to his every desire, when Hyde walks out from the bathroom and freezes when he sees me without a stitch of clothes on and Foster's face buried between my thighs.

"Ah—"

"Shit," I squeal as I try to pull away from Foster's very skilled tongue.

"Get out, Hyde. Right. Now!" Foster growls as he moves to block Hyde's view of my extremely exposed lady parts.

Hyde whips around to leave but turns back. Oh, for the love of the goddess, I don't think I have ever been so mortified in my life. I also wonder if he has a death wish because Foster's glare has turned murderous, but it seems he only has a request.

"Could you maybe slide down a couple of chairs because that's where I normally sit?" Foss grabs the first thing his hand comes into contact with and launches the glass at his head to get his ass moving out of the bar so he can finish what he started. His intention wasn't to hurt Hyde; it seems he doesn't like to be disturbed when buried between my thighs.

I try to sit up, realizing how bad of an idea this is, but his hand on my belly halts any thought of me ending our encounter.

"I'm not done," He growls before pushing my legs apart again.

When his tongue flattens against me, dragging it slowly over my wet folds, I bite my lip to stop the moan he is trying to force from me. He is licking my pussy like he was born to do this.

Savoring me like I am the sweetest of honey. Sticky, sweet, hot, golden, and straight from the hive.

My gaze moves down to watch him as he kisses my clit. When he catches me watching him, he pulls back, making me shiver as I see my excitement glistening on his lips from his blissful ministrations.

"Do you enjoy watching me devour this delicious pussy, Shay?" My face heats, knowing he's right. It turns me on watching him. I simply didn't intend for him to know this.

Lights flash across my line of sight as he pushes his tongue inside me, and I feel the orgasm building. Bringing me closer to the brink. With his tongue still buried inside me, his thumb finds my clit circling it but refusing to touch me the way I need. Refusing to push me over the edge as his moan hums along my core straight to my clit.

"Foster, please."

"My mate doesn't beg. She demands. But no, beautiful, I won't fuck you because when you come, I want every drop of that sweet release on my tongue. I want to taste it all. My plan is to consume you like a starved man." With each of his declarations, my clit throbs, and I wiggle, trying to put his thumb where I want it.

He kisses my thighs before returning to my center, slick and dripping wet for him. His tongue dances across my clit while his fingers find my nipples hard and begging for his touch. When his tongue slides back inside me, I lose all control as the climax he wants to taste explodes around him.

Once he has every drop I give him licked clean, he pulls me off the bar before he bends me over the table. Hearing him sliding his pants down has my clit pulsing as I try to prepare myself for what he wants to do.

My heart is racing, my breathing is fast, and when I feel his cock rubbing against me, I jump.

"Calm down, sweetheart." I exhale when his cock slides inside my pussy rather than my ass as he threatened until I quickly realize why he did this when he pulls out, and I feel him pressed against my ass. He pushes in one slow inch at a time, causing me to suck in a deep breath as every muscle tightens up, prepared for the pain I fully expect will happen.

"Relax, babe. I promise you'll like it if you relax."

"And if I don't?" I try not to sound like a scared little girl, but I have no clue what to expect. If it hurt when he fucked me for the first time, this will probably be worse.

"Then I'll stop." He pushes again, and the groan he releases when fully seated inside me causes a moan of my own. "So fucking tight."

His fingers dip inside me, and the sensation of him fucking my ass and pussy has me wiggling with pleasure.

"Shay, stay still. I'm trying really fucking hard to rein Shadow in." He stops moving, which makes me cry out my frustration. After what I imagine was him forcing Shadow to submit, he returns to thrusting his hips at a punishing pace. He slams into me as his fingers push me over the edge. I come harder than ever, coating his fingers and the inside of my legs.

He brings his fingers to his mouth, licking the after-effect of my orgasm from them, but even with him doing this, when he slams his hand next to my face, I can still smell the musk of my arousal on them.

"I don't know what I love more, fucking you or devouring you," the timbre of his husky voice tells me he's close to finding his release. I groan, wiggling my ass. This is the last thing he needs as he howls while spilling inside me.

His lips against my back send another shiver coursing through me as we work to bring our breathing and heart rate back down. When he pulls out of me, the warm come of his orgasm trickles down my legs, mixing with my own.

"I can't believe we just did that."

"What, me fucking you in the middle of Stooges or me fucking that sweet ass of yours?"

"Well, both."

"Keep in mind, sweetheart, if you hadn't tested me with those sexy as sin fucking panties, you never would have found yourself thoroughly fucked right now."

"Lesson learned."

"I hope not."

"Why?"

"I rather enjoy ravaging you whenever I want," he says, turning me over to smash his mouth against mine.

And just like that, my pussy pulses with excited need.

Episode Ninety-Seven: Answer

Atlas

I SLAM MY phone down on the bar, cursing under my breath. Five minutes ago, I would have said this was a good fucking day. I was in a right proper mood. Denver and I got in an hour ride this morning. Madge made my favorite meal, and we were supposed to meet Foster and Finch for a game of pool later tonight.

Yeah, it was a great fucking day until Mick had to call and ruin it all.

"Madge, I have to take a run up to Denver."

"Did something happen?"

"One of the new recruits decided the club needed more money and thought pushing drugs through the club was the best way of achieving this."

"You have to be kidding me." I exhale my frustration, knowing the trip will be anything but short. I have to get rid of the evidence, manage the police, take care of the gang he put my club in bed with, and clean fucking house. Thank god Mick called me right away.

The last thing I need is the damn cops breathing down my neck or investigating one of my chapters. Especially when the Vanguard is still out there looking for us. Well, us isn't the right word; they're looking for Denver, but they know if they find me, he'll be close by.

If they take him back, I can't imagine he'll be alive for long. Ayaan will make sure of that shit. The more I look into things, I know Ayaan isn't working alone. Someone else is backing him. I don't know who yet, but I plan to figure it out soon.

I'm pissed that whoever wanted my dad's throne so damn bad didn't have the guts to face him in battle. Everyone knows if you challenge my father, he'll meet you head-on. He was never the kind of king who sent others to do what he himself was unwilling to handle. This means the asshole who wanted his throne would have faced him and him alone.

"Want me to come?" Denver doesn't want me to leave him behind, but we both know the Vanguard was last seen close to the chapter I'm heading to. So, for this reason alone, we both know he needs to stay here. Foster will conceal Denver within his pack if they show up in Lake while I'm gone. This is a luxury we won't have on the road.

"Nah, I need you here to handle shit if it trickles back to us." He glares at me, knowing this isn't the reason, but he can't argue his point. Not with half the club members present and none of them knowing who we really are.

"I'll go, Cap," Tex interjects. Texas is a massive mountain of a man whose bulk is only rivaled by the size of his heart. This big bastard would rather buy you a beer than take your head off. Which makes most of the men who run afoul of him happy

Marcelle Valentine

to hear. Make no mistake though, if you push him too hard, he isn't completely opposed to beating your ass.

"I can handle it—"

"Bullshit. Either you take Tex or me, but one of us is going," Denver snaps, cutting me off. There is no point in fighting Denver on this. If I want him to stay here, I must make some concessions. I give my answer with a nod as we head toward the door.

Even though the day is frigid, Tex doesn't bitch like some of the other guys would have. He keeps his mouth shut, his head down, and never once does he ask me to pull over. This is a good thing because I had no intention of making any stops on my way to Denver. And because he rode like the devil was chasing him, we made good time and pulled into the lot a couple of hours later.

Mick already knew I was coming, so I gave him one specific order: the recruit was to be there when I arrived. The club bailed his ass out of jail after I gave my consent. I can't fix this shit if his ass is sitting inside a cell. Well, I can, but there would be more questions than I care to answer.

Storming into the club, I slide the skull cap I wore more for show than anything else into my pocket.

"Where the fuck is he?" I ask the first member I see, Badger. A weaselly little fucker who happens to be a damn genius. A word my kind does not toss around lightly.

"In church." I nod as I head into the room they hold their meetings in.

"I don't answer to you, asshole. You don't fucking run things around here." I growl, hearing this bastard back talking the man I left in charge of this chapter. I don't know who the fuck he thinks he is, but I will not tolerate any recruit coming in here disrespecting a man who has more than proven his loyalty.

"No, but you will fucking answer to me." His head snaps in my direction. When he realizes I'm the one standing here, all his cocky confidence slips away, leaving fear in its wake.

"Hey Atlas, I didn't know you were coming," he stammers, shifting in his chair.

"You take it upon yourself to associate my club with drugs. You aren't smart enough to do it without getting busted the first fucking run you make. You brought cops, a rival MC, a wanna-be gangster into our world, and you wonder why the fuck I had to travel up here."

"Atlas—"

"Shut the fuck up, asshole. What's the damage, Mick?"

"Well, I have a meeting set up with the other MC. The drugs are gone... confiscated by our local narc unit when they arrested this moron. The cops will be harder to get off our back, and the guy who set up the deal is long gone."

"Take Tex and the dumbass with you to the meetup. He can answer for this shit, but after that, he's out." The dumbass attempts to interject, but Tex shoves him back down in the chair before lifting his finger to his lips to silence him.

"Will do."

"I'll handle the cops.

"Alright."

"I don't want to hear about anyone else doing this shit. Am I making myself clear on this subject?"

"Crystal." I walk over and crack the cap on the bottle of scotch. With the first taste, I let my shoulders relax. Based on Mick's recounting, with any luck, the Vanguard will not investigate this shit. As typical as this may appear for an MC, there is nothing to suggest supernatural involvement; I have recently been apprised they know we are hiding among one. They merely have not discovered which one or where. This shit may clue them in, which only serves to piss me off more.

"I think you should know one more thing."

"What's that?" I ask, gripping the bottle tighter.

"The one who set up the deal was that dude your buddy was looking for."

"Which guy?" I asked through my clenched jaw and gritted teeth. I have a pretty goddamn good idea whom he is talking about, and if I'm right, then this fucker just brought me into their pack shit. Something he will regret doing.

"Travis."

"Mother Fucker!"

Episode Ninety-Eight: That's Alpha To You

Max

TRAVIS TOSSES THE bag of cash on my desk before he helps himself to my glass of whiskey. I guess our propensity to share does not end with women. Although I have to say I don't mind sharing any of my women with him, my whiskey, not so much.

When he tries to hand me back the pilfered contents with only a sip left in the glass, I wave him off, opting to do what he should have done to begin with... pay a visit to my liquor cabinet. I pour a generous serving into a fresh glass, only to have Trav clink the ice in his stolen one.

"Do I look like your fucking maid?" The challenging tone I reply with has him wisely removing his ass from my chair to get it himself. Who said the boy wasn't smart? I top my drink off before returning to my chair to prop my feet up on the desk.

Marcelle Valentine

"Everything go okay?" I ask, lifting the glass to my lips to inhale the nutty, oaky scent, but I find the undertones of licorice and grains most appealing about my preferred brand of amber addiction.

"Yeah, the dumb fucker practically came in his jeans when I showed him the blow."

"You get the price we wanted?"

"More. He was so antsy to get his hands on it; I figured he'd jump at whatever price I wanted."

"Good job, little brother."

"How long before this Atlas dude figures out we're the ones who set up his MC?"

"He already knows," I tell him as I help myself to another drink.

"How the hell do you know that?"

"Because no matter how hard that big bastard tries to blend in as a mortal man, he is anything but. He knew within hours of you dropping the dime on his club's *fabricated dirty dealings*."

"I was still in Denver then."

"Yeah. So?"

"You didn't think to warn me."

"Stop crying like a bitch. He didn't catch you. Hell, he didn't have any idea you were still there. What about the cops?"

"It's not a fucking stretch for an MC to be involved in drug running, Max. Those useless fuckers ate that shit up and begged for more," he responds as he finishes his drink, but when Travis slams the glass down on my desk, it only takes my eyes slowly lifting to his for him to understand he's not fucking leaving it there. He can shake his head all he damn wants. I've already told his ass once I'm not a goddamn maid. I wait until he cleans it and returns to his seat before I continue questioning him.

"Alright, so with this Atlas guy neck-deep in shit for a minute, can we get what I want now?"

"Soon."

"When? When are we going to claim what belongs to me, Max?"

"When I'm sure Foster will be too busy to notice. You get the blow back?"

"What do you think?"

"Well, where is it?"

"I gave it to Tosh."

"What the hell, Travis. Why in the fuck would you give that bitch five keys of our coke?"

"Because I could. If you didn't want me handing it off, you should have got it your damn self." Our mother always told me Travis wasn't the sharpest tool in the shed, but this takes the cake. It just proves how truly stupid he is.

I growl as I slam my chair down on all fours. "Let's go, dumbass."

*****

I don't wait for her to invite me in; I don't have to. But hindsight being twenty-twenty, I probably should have since the second I slam the door open to enter her room, I find her with a purple vibrator buried inside her as she plucks at her nipples like they are a goddamn guitar.

"What the fuck, Max. Ever heard of knocking?"

"Yeah, I just didn't want to."

"This is my damn room."

"And it's my damn pack, so why don't you wrap it up, Princess, and get me my shit."

"What shit?" she asks as she pulls a robe around her. In reality, calling this thing a robe is ridiculous since part of her ass is still in view, and I can see her taut nipples through it.

"Don't play fucking games with me, Natashia. Get my blow and get it now."

Tosh stomps over to her closet to pull the bag out. A closet. Five fucking keys stashed in a damn closet. The look I give Travis over my shoulder doesn't leave any room for misinterpretation of how pissed off I am about this situation. With any luck, he may actually realize how stupid he was for giving her my blow.

When I try to take the bag from her after she strolls back with it in hand, she pulls it behind her, "What's the hurry, Maximus? Why don't you stay awhile? You could always replace my toy with something better. Possibly your favorite plaything."

She runs her hand across my dick. You know, just in case I didn't understand her not-so-subtle come-on. I grin as I snake my arms around her waist. With her lust-filled eyes shining bright, I lean closer; her triumphant grin suggests she believes she's won. When my lips are a hair's breadth away from hers, I snatch the bag before muttering, "Not interested. Maybe Trav will take you up on your offer."

I don't wait for their responses as I amble out of the room with my bag of coke slung over my shoulder; after all, it's the only reason I came here. I gather from her huffed exhale she's not happy with my answer, but when she follows this up with a shrill squeal, I would have to say Travis is delighted to oblige.

"No, Rose, this is our damn pack, and we have a right to know." More trouble. Damn, this is becoming a shit day. More so as I watch this prissy she-wolf march directly toward me, blocking my path forward. "I want to know what the hell you're doing with this pack. What kind of shit are you getting us wrapped up in?"

"Truly?"

"Damn right. I demand you tell me," she snarls, which causes a slight chuckle from me. I'll give it to her; she's got balls. In fact, she's the only damn wolf in this pack who has displayed any. This doesn't mean I'll let her get away with it.

"And you are."

"Ophelia. I would expect the Alpha of my pack to know that."

"Hmm. Well… Ophelia. I am the Alpha of this pack, and the reason I don't know your fucking name is that I don't give a shit about you. You're no one." She tries to interrupt until I release my hold over Nexus. His growl silences her immediately.

"Furthermore, what I'm doing with this pack is above your pay grade." I motioned for the sentinel who followed me. When Rose screams, her girlfriend whips around, growling at me.

"Let her go!"

"No."

"Rose didn't do anything. I'm the one who made the demands, not Rosie."

I stroll closer, wanting to make sure she doesn't miss a word of what I have to say before giving her my response, "Yeah, but something tells me watching her suffer will hurt you a whole lot more than if I tortured you."

Three of my sentinels converge on her as the rest circle Rose. I'll give it to the girl; she puts up one hell of a fight. But she's no match for my guards. She bucks, hoping to break their hold while they drag a crying Rose away.

"You fucking piece of shit!" she screams.

"That's Alpha piece of shit to you, Ophelia," I tell her as I stroll away with my coke slung over my shoulder.

Marcelle Valentine

Episode Ninety-Nine: Add Another Thing to the List

Shay

*H*AD SOMEONE TOLD me a year ago I would be happy and free, with friends who genuinely care about me, not to mention a mate I'm over the moon for, I would have told them they were nuts, but here I am, living the life I always hoped for.

Memories have replaced those dreams, and I must tell you, memories are so much sweeter than a fantasy ever could be. Unless the fantasy becomes a reality courtesy of a hot Alpha, who likes to say the sun only rises because of me. Corny. Yeah, I know, but it makes me a little weak in the knees whenever he whispers it to me.

Last night after he thoroughly fucked me happy, I almost told him I loved him, but I chickened out at the last second. We have a fantastic thing going on here, and I don't aspire to be the one to screw it up. I know he cares for me but loves... well, that's another matter altogether.

"Wanna share what has that grin covering your face?" Ness asks as she bumps my shoulder.

"No. You don't want to know what I'm thinking about."

"Oh. So my cousin has a starring role in the grin." I almost burst out laughing when she wobbles her head while wiggling her eyebrows.

"Foster seems to take the lead in most of my thoughts anymore."

"So, when are you two going to make it all official? I say it's past time you two marked one another."

"Um, probably never," I abruptly reply as I start my trek back across pack land.

"What? Why in the hell not?" How do I explain I don't have the foggiest idea of how the whole marking thing works. Yet another thing I should have learned while growing up, but no one felt I needed to know. Adela all but told me I would never be claimed. She wouldn't allow it. Wouldn't permit my traitorous blood to be passed on to another pup. When I died, so would it.

Don't get me wrong, I understand the basic mechanics of it, but not the important shit.

"Does Foster know you don't want to be mated to him?" I can't blame her for being pissed. Foss might be her cousin by blood, but acknowledging him as her brother would be more accurate. And I don't know any she-wolf who would be okay with some chick screwing with her brother's head, especially with no intention of making things official.

When I continue walking without offering her any explanation, she grabs my arm, forcing me to look at her.

"You don't owe me anything, Shay, but you owe it to Foster to be honest with him. If you don't plan to declare yourself my cousin's mate, then you need to break the bond so he can—"

"I don't want to break our bond," I interject in a rush.

"You can't have it both ways. Foster deserves better."

"I know." When I interrupt her this time, her expression shifts from confusion to annoyance if the pursed-lipped, lowered brow appearance is anything to go by. I get it. She may like me, but she loves him and is merely using caution. I would do the exact same thing if the roles were reversed.

"Then—"

"I don't know how, Ness," I tell her, dropping my voice so only she can hear my confession.

"How to what?"

"Mark my mate," I say as my cheeks heat from my response.

"What? How is that possible?"

"Ness—my pack—they... No one ever...." Her eyes soften as it finally dawns on her what I'm trying to tell her.

"Taught you. No one ever taught you about the mating ceremony."

"You have to know how much I care about Foster, and if I could... if I knew how—"

"You would. Because you love him. Don't you?"

"I—I," as much as I want to confess my feelings, I can't seem to force the words up my throat and out of my mouth. I'm afraid there is a genuine possibility I may not be capable of saying them, and if I can't, will Foster one day give up on me?

"It's alright, Shay." Damn it if the pity isn't back in her eyes again. I wish they would stop looking at me like this. Thankfully, she hides the emotion replacing it with one of certainty, and this one makes me afraid.

"I think it's time for a girl's night. With wine. Lots and lots of wine, snacks, and plenty of boy talk."

"Ness—"

"Don't you Ness me. It's time for you to learn everything the assholes from your last pack didn't tell you. Brady better count his lucky stars that I don't hate him anymore."

"Speaking of boy talk, what's happening with you and Brady?"

"Nothing." She says as she loops her arm through mine and pulls me in the direction I know our mates are sparring against each other.

"I wouldn't call that kiss the other day… nothing."

"Oh, shush, Shay." Her attempt at sounding annoyed would be much more believable if she wasn't sporting a mammoth grin.

She doesn't stop dragging me along until she hauls my ass into the complex. The cheers echoing off the walls confirm Brady and Foster are still at it. As hard as Ness is dragging me in the direction of the sparring ring, I have to say she's eager to see a certain blonde-haired, hazel-eyed mate. I can't say I blame her because the second we enter, seeing Foster's bare chest with a thin layer of sheen from his workout covering his frame has me captivated as well.

Brady was always a good fighter. Hell, he was one of the best at our previous pack, but under Foster's direction, he has become damn near unstoppable. But even after all the extra practice, he is still no match for my mate, especially since Foss easily tosses him aside or plain outmaneuvers him whenever he tries.

"You have to be faster than that, little brother," Foster informs with a laugh.

90

Brady charges him again but comes in too high, making it much too easy for Foster to twist and cage his head between his bicep and the chest that I enjoy running my fingers over. Or tongue. Or my breast. Let's make this simple. I love touching every part of him with any part of me.

When I was busy fantasizing about everything I would prefer his body to be doing now rather than fighting his brother, Foster realized I had entered. And when my eyes roam from the shorts slung precariously low on his hips to a muscled, golden chest up to his face, I find his focus on me. When he winks at me, I can't stop the blush from creeping along my cheeks because it tells me one thing... he knows what I was thinking about.

And the cheeky bastard enjoys it.

Episode One Hundred: One Day

Foster

I MAY HAVE had this fight squarely in the bag, but the second I saw Shay standing there with her eyes appreciating the sight of my body, I lost focus, and Brady tried to take advantage of it. Fortunately, he comes in a little too high, granting me the opportunity of not ending up on my ass with my mate here to witness the entire thing.

Rather than tossing him aside, I let him save face in front of my cousin. How could I not? I believe I have already proven myself to Shay, while Brady still fights for this with Ness. Her resolve is crumbling one piece at a time. I can see him winning her over.

I know you may find this hard to believe, but I'm actually pulling for my brother. The longer I'm around him, the more I like him, and while Finn will always be the brother I chose, it's not horrible having one that shares my same lineage.

This doesn't mean I'll let him win to impress my sweet little bear of a cousin. He has to take me down fair and square.

After our fight today, I'll tell him how I always block his attack from the right side. If I want to help strengthen him, it's my job as his brother to point out his weaknesses. Even though every tip I give him only makes him harder to beat. At this rate, it's only a matter of time before he wins.

Let me fill you in on a little secret... I look forward to the day he does.

He fakes his rush to my left, only to drop to his knees to take out my legs. Using his back for leverage, I kick my legs out as he reaches for them and flip myself behind him. I told him that once he could beat me as a man, it would be our wolves' turn to battle it out. I don't know if his wolf is as big a pain in the ass as mine or as big of a smartass, but if he is, then Shade must be driving him as crazy as Shadow is with me.

Shay distracts me briefly, allowing Brady to land one good hit. I run my hand over my lip, only to find a trace of blood smeared along my fingertips.

"Gotcha, Foss."

"Even the sun shines on a dog's ass once in a while."

"Seems like it is burning bright on Shade and my backside today, then." His crazed raucous laughter echoes around us, sending up roars of cheers from some and jeers from others.

"That it is... you can thank my mate for bringing said ass the sunbeams," I grunt, as I return the favor. His laugh disappears the instant his head snaps back. Before he can recover, I lunge, easily taking his legs out from under him. I don't hesitate to wrap up this sparring match when he topples over. There is someone else I would rather exert myself with. One petite, blonde-haired, blue-eyed beauty named Shay.

"You couldn't give me one? You know, throw your brother a bone since his newly discovered mate is watching."

"What good do you think it would do? Ness would know, and she'd never let you live it down. Think of it as an act of compassion saving you from a lifetime of 'remember when Foster let you win?' Trust me, baby brother, you don't want that."

"Well, could you at least cut out the baby brother shit?" I laugh as I pull him to his feet before clapping my hand on his shoulder.

"Not making any promises."

With the exhibition over, most of the pack returns to whatever they were doing prior to discovering who was sparring. Shay and Ness weave through the crowds leaving the arena. As are Finn, Maggie, and Sadie.

"Bro, he took you down hard. Word of advice: don't try to embarrass him in front of the Shayster."

"Obviously," Brady mumbles as he rubs his jaw.

"Don't let them get under your skin, Brady. I think you held your own." Shay challenges, looking at me from the corner of her eye, almost daring me to disagree. I am so going to enjoy punishing that sweet little ass of hers.

"So now that we've all watched Foss thoroughly tromp Brady's ass, what do you all want to do now? I say we head over to Stooges; maybe Brady can win back some of his dignity in a round of darts," Finch says as he points from one person to the next.

"Hard pass. The only thing I want to do right now is to grab a quick shower before tending to my bruised ego with a bottle of bourbon from my brother's liquor cabinet." Brady's comment causes a chuckle from everyone around us except

Ness, who is smiling at him like he just broke away another brick in the wall she's built up.

"I promised mom I would help her today," Ness mumbles, followed by an over-exaggerated groan. I guess she would rather go drinking than bake cookies. Too bad for her because I won't let her dip out on Aunt Claire.

"I supposed the way you two are looking at one another, you're not coming either?" The only response from Shay and I are our beaming grins.

"Well, ladies, it looks like it's just us."

"I could use a drink," Sadie confirms. Finch and his flirty self drapes an arm over their shoulders, leading them out of the training facility.

When Shay realizes we are alone, she slowly circles away from me. Did she really believe I would let her get far? I can't help but appreciate the game of cat and mouse she is playing as I stalk in her direction.

"Did you have fun today, Foster?"

"Not as much as I plan on having with you."

"You plan on showing me all your best moves?" With a playful glint in her eye, she teases, her bottom lip clenched between her teeth.

"Stop running, and you'll know."

"If you want me, handsome, you have to catch me." With her challenge issued, she moves away from me. And, like my response to Brady, I waste no time rushing her. She squeals as I toss her over my shoulder. I plan to show her whatever she wants to see, but we need privacy for the things I plan to do.

"Gotcha."

"That you do. The question is, what do you plan on doing with me?"

Marcelle Valentine

"You and your naughty little wolf are about to find out."

She sucks in a deep breath as I turn to leave. As the scent of her arousal surrounds us.

Episode One Hundred One: Confession

Foster

As I STORM out of the complex, the cool air does nothing to dampen my growing desire. Honestly, it doesn't stand a chance with the way my mate is wiggling and the scent of her escalating excitement. How could it?

I briefly hear Ian saying something, but he stops when he sees Shay. "Oh, for Pete's sake."

"Sorry, Ian," she replies with a giggle when I smack her ass. I don't stop until I slam the door closed with my foot and let my mate slide down the front of me. My lips smash against hers as I back her into the bathroom.

"What are you doing?"

"Taking a shower," I murmur, with my lips skimming hers.

"Hurry up then," she replies with a nip to the lip still brushing against hers.

"Who said I plan to take it alone, beautiful."

Marcelle Valentine

"What?" Not one to give her any opportunity to pull away, I slip my hands under her perfect ass as I enter the bathroom. She can feign her objection all she wants; the flash of excitement I find in her eyes when I yank her shirt over her head confirms her protests are more show than anything else.

Shay takes me by surprise when she pushes me away and drops to her knees in front of me. She clears her throat before removing my shorts. My body immediately responds when she runs her tongue over her soft, full lips. The thought of sliding into her mouth causes my dick to jump eagerly.

My heart hammers inside my chest as I wait for her to decide what she wants to do. I can tell you this much waiting is not what I want to do. What I want is to knot my fingers in her long locks as I take her mouth for the first time. But I won't do that. As much as I want to slowly slide between those fucking beautifully parted lips... no matter how much my body and wolf are pushing me to do what I have thought about countless times... I wait for her to decide.

When she slides her tongue over the lips, still swollen from our kiss, I question if she is doing this on purpose. My naughty little vixen is playing with fire, and I'm not sure she is ready for the consequences of her taunting.

Fuck! Shay either needs to let me fuck her, or she needs to follow through with what she started because seeing her on her knees, mouth inches from my cock, breasts out on full display, is damn near painful.

Her gaze slowly lifts to meet mine, and I find the same yearning I imagine rivals my own in those beautiful blue eyes that I would give a thousand lives for. I can't tell if the lip she has held tightly between her teeth is a sign of her own arousal or her inhibitions regarding what she plans to do. It doesn't matter because whichever reason has her torturing it is fucking hot as sin.

"Beautiful, I am trying really fucking hard to let you decide, but I'm losing the battle. If you persist with teasing me with that fucking tongue and those lips, I'm going to—"

She doesn't allow me to finish as her tongue runs the length of my shaft, and I can't tell who growls louder, Shay or me. That is until she pulls me into her mouth and the most enraptured pleasure courses through me. The groan I give her as I grasp her hair is significantly louder than her moan. She has bewitched me and could give a shit less. I will happily worship at the altar of Shay for the rest of my days.

*****

Fuck, for someone who was a virgin until recently, she knows how to bring me to the brink in a matter of minutes. She increases the speed and force of her suctions. As much as I am trying to let her run this show, my hips have taken on a mind of their own as they pivot to meet Shay's movements.

"Shay," I try to warn her, but she does not relent, and the moan she pulls out of me as I lose myself in her mouth is more animal than man. She doesn't hesitate... she doesn't pull back. No, she moans as I spill the last of my climax. Her tongue caressing my cock is one of the hottest things any woman has ever done to me until she pulls back to lick the head of my dick, and the rest of my come away. Damn, I want her to do it again right after I dine on her delicious fucking pretty pussy.

Yanking her to her feet, I smash my mouth to hers, only long enough to back her against the wall. Once there, I drop to one knee, lift her legs over my shoulder, and kiss the pussy I plan to destroy. Her moans, groans, and writhing prove I am accomplishing what I set out to do.

Her hand flies up when I bury three fingers inside her while I flick my tongue over the engorged nub she is desperate for me to suck into my mouth. I assume she is doing this to find something to anchor herself with, but the only thing she accomplishes is accidentally smacking the shower head aside as my free hand glides up to her perfect tits to play with her rock-hard nipples.

"Foster. Fuck-fuck-fuck."

"Soon, beautiful, but not until I taste the sweetest fucking thing in the world."

"Which is," her pants are coming in ragged bursts as she moves closer to her orgasm.

"Your come."

"Oh my goddess," her voice is tinged with equal parts desire and embarrassment from my confession. But it doesn't stop her from giving me what I have thought about all day, and I devour every drop she provides.

Licking her clit once more, I drop her legs to kiss my way up to her waiting mouth.

"So much for your shower," she says with an adorable giggle.

"I'll take this over a shower any day, beautiful." She pulls back, letting her blue eyes assess me, but the smile she grants us melts away the final bit of my reserve.

Everything becomes clear. I know this woman is everything Shadow and I have ever needed. Everything we will ever want. And not just because she is my mate, but because she is everything my heart has been missing. Every piece of the puzzle, and I need her to know it.

"I love you, Shay."

Her eyes grow wide as a soft whisper tumbles past her kissable lips. "What?"

"Marry me."

*****

Shay

"Wha-what did you just say?"

"I said I love you, Shay, and I have for a long time. Of course, I want you to be my wife."

"But that would make me the Luna. I don't wanna be the Luna."

"Beautiful, you don't have to do anything you don't want to do. But I happen to believe you would be a fantastic Luna to our pack."

"Your pack."

"No, babe, I got it right the first time. This is our pack."

"I never officially joined the pack."

"I think that's a little redundant. Don't you?"

"A rogue wolf officially joining a pack? Ah, no. I think it's kind of required."

"You're not rogue because your status in this pack goes without saying. Yet if you want the whole shindig, I can arrange it. Hell, Nessie will be in her damn glory planning the event."

"I-I. Oh, goddess... I think... No, I know I need to sit down." Foster smiles as he scoops me into his arms to carry me into the other room. Once he places me on the bed, I instantly begin with my nervous habit of gnawing on my bottom lip, completely lost in my thoughts.

Marcelle Valentine

For the next five minutes, I tell him all the reasons he should not want to marry me. Why he shouldn't love me, why I would make a horrible Luna, but every reason I give, he rebuffs, telling me why he does.

"Shay, it's really hard to concentrate on your fears when you're naked. The only thing I can think about is sliding between those soft thighs and fucking you until you see things my way." Holy shit, I completely forgot I was sitting here without a stitch of damn clothes on. Now I know why he grinned every time I flung my arms around because I can only imagine my tits were bouncing all over like a bunny on crack.

"Foster, be serious." I chastise as I yank a sheet around me, but he's there almost as quick to pull it away.

"Oh, I am serious. Let's see if I can make that happen."

"What happen?"

"Fuck you until you see things my way," He informs as he crawls over me before sliding between my legs. The second he pushes his dick inside me, my core clenches tight, and as much as I hate to admit this, it seems he can make it happen. Oh, goddess! He can make it happen. I'll agree to everything and anything he wants as long as he continues sliding his cock into me like this.

Mate. Moon purrs happily.

Who knew a wolf could do that?

Episode One Hundred Two: On the Edge

Brady

I SWEAR, I think Ness is trying to torture me. There is no other way to describe it. One second, she is kissing me in front of the entire bar. The next she refuses to give me the time of day. And today, while I was sparring with Foster, she looked excited. So you can imagine what I thought when she showed up at my door shortly after I arrived home. Especially since she made a production telling everyone she had to help her mom.

Apparently, my hope was for nothing because what I thought she came here for couldn't be further from the truth since she is back to pretending we are nothing more than friends. Movie watching, popcorn eating, no kissing, no cuddling, or screwing friends. Ordinarily, I would be happy with anything she wanted to give, but Shade is harder to push down after a workout like the one Foster put us through today. I admit to being slightly jealous because I imagine watching a movie is not what he's doing right now with his mate. Not that I want Shay. All those feelings I had vanished the second I found my Nessie.

Shay told me it would happen. I honestly didn't believe her. I mean, I cared for Shay. A lot. I couldn't imagine anything coming between us or rivaling how I felt about her. Damn, was I fucking wrong because Ness's happiness is everything to me.

As much as I enjoy seeing her in my bed as we watch a movie, there are so many other things I would rather be doing with her right now. I try to hold in the low groan as I shift to lean further against the headboard.

"Everything okay?"

"Yeah. I'm sore from working out so hard today, but it's fine. Nothing a long...." This next part is merely a thought, not something I voice to Nessie, ice cold, "shower and a good night's sleep can't fix."

"I can go if you're not in the mood for company."

"Why would you think I don't want you here?"

"You said—"

"I said I was sore, not dying. I enjoy spending time with you, and even if every muscle in my body hurts like hell, I would still prefer you to be here. Besides, who would womansplain the movie to me if you left?"

"That is not a term."

"Oh, I see. So mansplaining is—"

"A thing. Womansplaining isn't." She interrupts as she looks at me from the corner of her eye. I think she's taunting me.

"It is now, and I'm willing to bet there's an entire populace of men out there who would agree with me. Especially if they ever met you. Womansplainer."

"You asshole," she laughs as she sits up to hit me with the pillow she was using.

I let her get in a couple of good hits before wrestling the pillow away from her. Somehow, we end up with her on the bottom and me on top with my arms caging her between them. I sink down to my elbows, which allows me to push a strand of hair away from her face before I lower myself to kiss the lips I have been focused on all night.

"We should finish the movie."

As hard as it is to resist, I do the impossible and collapse onto the bed next to her.

"Are you mad?"

"Nope, just trying to reel Shade in," I confess.

"You're really okay with waiting until I'm ready?"

"For you? Absolutely."

"Why? I've been nothing but a bitch to you."

I push up on my elbow because I want her to look me in the eye as I tell her this honest truth, "Because you are worth waiting for."

"Even if we never do anything?"

"I'd wait. But I don't think we can any longer classify our relationship as platonic."

"Why not?"

"The kiss you planted on me at Stooges was anything but friendly. Scorching, hot-as-hell, verging on X-rated, but platonic, no goddamn way."

"It didn't mean anything."

"Uh-huh."

"What? It didn't. You're making a mountain out of a molehill. Besides, it's not like you stopped me."

"Because I'm not a fucking idiot. And keep in mind, Nessie, you kissed me."

"Only to shut that cow up."

"You didn't have to keep kissing me after accomplishing your goal. You did because you liked it."

"Shut up," she says as she pushes me away. Laughing, I crawl back up to lean against the headboard, and she shifts so her head is lying in my lap. I also notice she doesn't pull away as I trail my fingers over the exposed skin on her neck and shoulder.

Every time my fingers glide across the space my wolf is desperate for us to mark her breathing increases. Even if she isn't ready to admit it yet, I think she likes me touching her as much as I enjoy doing it.

When she abruptly sits up to look at me, I reach out to run my thumb against her cheek. When she doesn't pull away, I move closer to kiss her, but she ends this idea when she leaps from my bed and saunters toward the bathroom. Goddess, this girl is going to be the damn death of me.

"Where are you going?"

"To take a shower."

"Right now? You want to take a shower right this second?"

"Yeah." With her confirmation, my head falls back against the headboard, and my eyes slip closed as I do my best to rein in the desire to claim her as much as get the erection she caused to relent.

I sense her standing on the threshold between my room and the bathroom. When I turn to look at her, she is standing there with nothing but her thong on. My confusion about why she would want to tease a man on the edge is short-lived when she says her next words. This one question sends a tidal wave of desire ripping through me and has me scrambling off the bed.

"Care to join me?"

Episode One Hundred Three: Dirty Deeds

Riona

AFTER MAKING SURE the little bitch who hasn't figured out Foster belongs to me has him occupied... I can only imagine what the pathetic little wallflower has to do to accomplish this... I slip onto pack land and race toward his cottage.

Thank you, Finch. Since he had no issue telling everyone at the bar, Foss and Shay wouldn't be coming.

I have to be careful not to cross paths with any of the wolves for several reasons. One, I haven't officially been accepted into the pack. Two, if a wolf finds me, they would have to bring me to the Alpha, which would end badly for me, or the beta, who I don't want to see again so soon. And three, which is the biggest reason: plausible deniability.

I want to sneak in, get the intel I want and get out with no one the wiser before I finish this little excursion by paying a visit to the wallflower's house. Thankfully, my wolf is smarter than most of the simpletons in every pack I have been a part of. Giving me an advantage. I'd almost feel bad for them if I gave a shit.

I know I am meant to be a Luna, and no one can tell me otherwise, especially not these whiny women who have their claws dug deep into the men I want. And while I haven't managed to convince the alphas I went after yet, I have a good feeling about Foster. He can pretend he isn't interested, but his wandering eyes prove otherwise.

His cottage wasn't hard to find. Especially since I can smell his woodsy scent out here. Still, I use caution rather than rush inside like my wolf wants so we can surround ourselves with his manly musk. Patience has never been my strong suit, but I have to ensure his damn cousin isn't inside. The entire world thinks I am nothing more than a beautiful moron, which is something I won't dispel. I allow them to believe this so I can watch and listen. You learn things when you keep your mouth shut and open your ears. For example, Finch tends to stay at Foster's place most nights.

This is why I didn't rush in because I overheard Foster and Finch talking during one of the many times I was listening. This intel may prevent me from stumbling in on a wolf who may believe I am here for him. As much as I could use the release, I don't want him to get any satisfaction... only me. He's not getting his rocks off inside my body. If he wants to go down on me, I'm good with it, but that's where it will end. Selfish? I know, and I simply don't care.

Besides, I don't have time for a full-on fuck fest. Not if I want to accomplish what I set out to do.

After I am confident no one is inside the house, I cautiously sneak in. What I am looking for is anything I can use to help me win him over. When I leave here and go to the wallflower's house, it will be to find anything to discredit her.

I systematically search room after room. The one thing that becomes clear is that he cares about his family and is big on honoring commitments. I can work with this.

Every room in his house displays his love and admiration for his aunt and cousins. I can't tell you how much I revel in the fact not one thing about Shay is present here. No photos, no mementos of their time together, nothing I would expect to find at a boyfriend's house if he was into her as much as he pretends to be.

The minute I enter Finch's room, I know it because his scent permeates the air surrounding me. Not to mention he is not as meticulous about his cleaning. Rifling through his clothes, I find some things I can use in his hamper. Items I plan to put to good use later.

The next room I enter is heavy with the aroma of that bitch who will become family after I marry Foster... Vanessa. Little Nessie needs to get on board with the new regime or get the fuck out of my future pack. I'll let her decide. If she chooses to stay with the Ash Rock pack, I will ensure she understands I will only permit it if she severs all ties with the wallflower.

It's not until I get to his bedroom that I relax enough to enjoy being in his house. His scent is heavier here than in any other room. I want to wrap myself in his manly aroma and live here for a while. As I stroll through the space, I allow my fingers to skim the surfaces and his clothes. When I find one of his shirts haphazardly tossed over the chair, I help myself to it. I figure I need it as much as he does.

I save his bed for last. I already told you I want to wrap myself in his scent; this is how I plan to do it. Stripping off my clothes, I slip between the sheets and bask in the smell surrounding me. The more I lay here, the more turned-on I become until my hand slips between my thighs to rub my soaking wet core. I suddenly wish Finch was here. He could replace my hand with his face while I fantasize it's Foster. It wouldn't be hard with his aroma surrounding us.

After I fully satisfied myself and left my musk in his bed for him to enjoy tonight, I reluctantly climbed out. If I didn't have one more stop, I would have stayed the night in his bed. I have no fear of him coming in and finding me here because I would ensure he enjoyed the show I would grant him. This thought brings another wave of heat pooling between my thighs. Damn, I can't wait until he finally gives in.

With his shirt slung over my shoulder, I vacate his house for the last time as a single wolf because when I walk out the next time I come here, it will be as his chosen mate.

*****

As I did with Foster's cottage, I cautiously observed the wallflower's house before letting myself in. I am not on a mission to find out what she wants or to leave my scent here for her to enjoy. No, I'm here for only one thing... to figure out how to get rid of her without Foster ever learning of my involvement.

How pathetic is it that this bitch doesn't have any personal effects here? Not one picture, mention, or remembrance of her dead mom or traitorous dad. Maybe she's just as embarrassed by them as any sane wolf would be or should be. Hell, knowing what they did, the bitch should be mortified.

111

First, I enter her bathroom to inspect what shampoo, conditioner, body wash, and perfume she uses. What I find doesn't surprise me. A low groan slips out as I toss the bottle back into the shower. Of course, this nobody would buy her hygiene products from the corner store. Why wouldn't she?

With this information stored, I move on to phase two. Driving a wedge between my mate and the bitch who doesn't want to see it. This is what I needed Finch's stuff for. Sheets, a shirt, and a pair of worn boxers. Fortunately, her bed and the one Finch sleeps on at Foster's, which Foss and I will discuss these living arrangements in detail after he claims me, are the same size.

I wonder how she will explain Finch's scent throughout her bed, especially after he finds his underwear between the sheets and his shirt beneath it. I said Foster is big on honor, and what he will be left to believe is about as dishonorable as you can get.

"Fucking his cousin. You should be ashamed of yourself, wallflower," I say to the empty room.

Before leaving, I help myself to a glass of wine and a snack. Reveling in the shitstorm I hope this will bring down on this bitch's head. I am pleased with myself knowing she will not be able to talk her way out of this and basking in the knowledge that the time I spent rolling around in Foster's bed will mask my scent enough that they won't easily detect it. In fact, unless they are looking for it, the dumb bitch will miss it altogether. And Foster will be so pissed he'll ignore it, but even if he doesn't, the aroma will be so pleasing he won't care.

Rather than returning to Uncle Seamus's house and listening to him bitch, I opt to head over to the bar. I can crash there for the night, and if Uncle Seamus wants to know what the hell I was doing, he'll never know I wasn't there all night.

This was my plan until I strolled through the door and came face-to-face with one very pissed-off uncle.

"Where the hell have ya been, and what are ya playin' at, Riona?"

Episode One Hundred Four: Tell Me The Truth

Shay

NAN'S SMILE NEVER seems to leave her face. She is even back in the kitchen cooking again. Not because she has to but because she wants to.

I also love seeing all the younger members of the pack surrounding her, waiting for a muffin fresh from the stove. Apparently, so does she, since the beaming smile she has worn since we arrived here morphs into sheer delight. Followed by giddy laughs for the kids to shoo.

If I did one thing right, it was releasing Nan and Moon from Half Crest. And now that Brady, Maggie, and, as unbelievable as this is to say, Sadie are here, I finally feel like I am right where I should be.

This is my pack. A pack I would give my life for. People I love and respect and a mate I am over the moon for. I still can't believe he loves me. Me. A shifter who has been told throughout my life how worthless I am. Especially when Foster could have just about any she-wolf he wanted. But he wants me. I suppose I probably should have told him I loved him too.

I know, stupid, right? Here I have a man I definitely love telling me he loves me, and rather than throwing my arms around him and professing the same, I freeze up. Three tiny words about how I feel could have replaced the one big word I am about to say. Stupid.

Foster knows. Moon tells me quietly.

It's not always about what you know, Moon. She doesn't have a response to this because she knows I'm right.

"You want to tell me why you are so quiet over there?"

"Sorry, Nan, I know I haven't been the best company today."

"So spill it, kiddo," she says as she hands me a muffin. Something she used to do when I was little, and she wanted to bribe me. I pick at the apple muffin as Nan leans on the counter, watching and waiting for me to tell her what's wrong.

"Foster. He um… I don't know…." Talking about this with anyone, even Nan, is hard. I know Nan. She'll take my confession to heart. If I admit to her, I don't know how to tell Foster I love him; she'll say if she had done better, I might have grown up knowing what it meant to be loved. She'll tell me it's as much her fault as the rest of them. But she would be mistaken because even when Nan was covering her own ass, she also did her best to protect me. Sometimes it worked, sometimes it didn't, but that's on Adela… not her.

"Oh hell yes, just in time," Ness triumphantly declares when she walks in and finds the freshly baked muffins on the counter.

"Already had one set aside for you," Nan says with a smile before turning to retrieve the muffin she stashed for Ness. Why would she do this? One word, Finch. I swear to the goddess he

Marcelle Valentine

has a sixth sense when it comes to Nan's baked goods. Hell, I'm astonished he isn't here already.

"I love you, Nan. Will you be my adopted grandma?" Ness may have said this in jest, but the sparkle in Nan's eyes confirms how much Nessie's comment meant to her. She never had a family of her own. She lived under not only Tobias's heavy-handed rule but his dad's before him, and neither one of these assholes felt their omega's were worth a shit. I can't tell you how overjoyed I was when Foster abolished the title right after we returned.

He doesn't like to be called Alpha, but he recognizes the need for someone to hold the role. I think this is partly what makes him such a great one. He doesn't view himself differently than any of the other wolves in the pack. His beta Ian, who keeps trying to step down, is exactly like Foster in this area. In fact, I think Ian may be one of the hardest-working betas I've ever met.

Ness eats her muffin and half of mine before asking, "You ready?"

"Ready for what?"

"Girl's day, baby. We're talking wine, snacks, wine, boy talk, and did I mention—"

"Wine? Yeah, I think you covered the wine part."

"Excellent. Glad to know we got the wine part well established," she replies with a huge grin.

"You seem overly happy today. Anything you want to share?" I ask, furrowing my brow until I am more squinting at her than looking.

"Can't a girl simply enjoy the day?"

"Uh-huh," I mutter, putting my hand on her forehead.

"I'm not sick, silly."

"Could have fooled me."

"It's just a fantastic day."

"Who the hell are you, and what have you done with my best friend?" I say as I tilt my head, trying to figure out what is different about her. Something is definitely off. My problem is I just can't put my finger on it.

"Well, what are we waiting for? Maggie and Sadie are already there."

"Already where?"

"Your place. Where else?" I start to ask how they got into my locked house, but what's the point? I'm sure it only took Nessie batting her lashes at Seamus until he agreed to give her access. Or... she stole my keys. My hand instantly shoots to where I thought my keys should be, only to discover them missing. My accusatory eyes drift over to the culprit, only to find her grinning like a damn Cheshire cat.

"But I was spending some time with—"

"Pish-posh, you go with your friends. 'sides I may have plans of my own," she declares before wiggling her eyebrows.

"No more excuses, Shay. Now get your ass in my car. Nan, it was a pleasure as always."

As bad as I felt ditching out on the conversation Nan thought we would have, something tells me that talking this over with Ness, Maggie, and Sadie will get me further. Of course, only after we work our way through most of the wine.

*****

Two hours later, we are sitting around my living room with more empty bottles of wine than plates around us. Why ruin a good buzz? This is what Maggie and Ness keep saying.

"Sorry I'm late," Sadie announces as she sweeps through the front door.

"Where the hell have you been?" Ness asks without slurring. An accomplishment for sure since she's had trouble with this for the last hour.

"I was... detained," Sadie says as she slips out of her jacket and snatches up a bottle to catch up with the rest of us. It's only after she has drunk two bottles and announced her lips are numb that Ness proceeds with the entire purpose of this night.

"Okay, so we're here today for a reason," Ness declares after clearing her throat, hoping to add an official tone to her statement. The problem is she slurs half of it and giggles with the rest.

"What, so this wasn't only about drinking copious amounts of alcohol, getting shit-faced, and waking up with a hangover tomorrow?" Sadie asks.

"No, this is lesson one on how to claim your mate."

"Huh?" Maggie's question is followed by her nose scrunching up as her eyes narrow. Okay, so Ness never told them I don't know how to officially claim my mate. Love her for keeping my secret... hate that I now have to confess it all over again.

"I think we all know how to claim our mate," Sadie says as she tries to plop back down in the chair, only to miss it and end up on her ass next to it. Amazingly, she saved her entire glass of wine. She takes a long drink to celebrate while the rest of us laugh.

After Sadie's Three Stooges moment, confessing my lack of knowledge about the marking ceremony was much easier. Maggie's sympathetic eyes instantly fall on me. Which are not as bad as the pity-filled ones, but not by much. Thankfully, Ness and Sadie's decision to act out what normally happens during the marking ceremony halted any apology she wanted to give.

And hearing Sadie's rendition of Foster was hilarious. Completely wrong, but funny as hell.

"I'm going to sink my fangs into this juicy fucking neck of yours, mate. After I'm confident the mark will chase away any asshole who wants to do the horizontal mambo with my future Luna, it'll be your turn. You and that hot ass of yours will return the favor. Then we'll fuck like rabid bunnies," Sadie says in the deepest tenor she can manage.

"Oh, Foster. Yes, bite me right here. Sink those big bad wolf fangs in my neck, you hunk of man meat." Ness's version makes my mouth fall open.

"I positively do not sound anything like that."

"This is my show. I can act it out any way I want."

"I have never said man meat in my life."

"Well, maybe you should," Ness declares.

They continue to act out how they claim the marking ceremony is done. I don't know how much I learned, but after Nessie tells me to relax and follow Foss's lead, I admit I feel better. About the ceremony and telling Foster the truth. Now I only need to figure out how to bring it up to him.

As the evening winds down, Maggie and Sadie claim the couch and the loveseat, leaving Ness and me to share my bed. Wandering into my bedroom, I immediately sense something is wrong. My heart leaps into my chest when I pick up a male scent that doesn't belong to Foster. With one cautious step after another, I back out of the room, my eyes shifting from one window to the next. Nervous energy consumes me, wondering who could have been in my house and whether they were still here.

But when Ness stumbles in, my heart moves from leaping to racing. "Did Finn sneak in when we weren't looking?"

"Finch?" It took my brain a second to catch up with what my senses knew the instant Ness said his name. Of course, the scent belongs to Finch. What I don't understand is why he would be in my house. Not that I care because if he had asked, I would have told him it was fine, but to come in without my permission or knowledge is kind of fucked up.

"Yeah, can't you smell him?" She moves toward the closet, figuring he must be hiding inside, but she only gets halfway to the door when she turns her head and sniffs the air. Abandoning the idea he's in there, she storms over to the bed, and her head whips in my direction the instant she arrives next to it. The look she gives me is anything but friendly.

"Why the hell was Finch in your bed?" I may have been okay with Finch coming to my place, but sleeping in my bed is definitely crossing the line.

"Shay?"

"I—I don't know, Ness."

"What do you mean you don't know?" she asks as she moves closer to the source of his aroma.

"I don't have any idea why he would be in here. I never told him he could, and he never asked." Ness resumes sniffing the air, trying to pinpoint where the source of the smell is heaviest. When she picks up a pillow to smell it, followed by the one on the other side, her angry gaze immediately settles on me.

"Why is Finn's scent all through your damn bed? Right next to your own."

"Ness, I'm telling you, I don't know why Finn was here." When she yanks the covers back, my heart morphs from racing to seizing when I see a pair of men's boxers in my bed. And one thing I know for sure is that they don't belong to Foster. But the fear only lasts a second when Ness holds up a shirt she found on the floor that I know belongs to Finn before fury replaces it. Did he bring someone to my house to have sex?

"Tell me the truth, Shay. Are you sleeping with my brother?"

"I can't believe you could even ask me that."

"It's a valid question. Are you fucking around on my cousin with my brother?"

"No. No, absolutely not! The only man I'm sleeping with is Foster," I growl. I don't know if I'm more pissed or hurt that she could actually think something so heinous about me. What kind of shitty person does she think I am?

Her eyes continue to assess me, and when they narrow, there is a second I believe she is preparing to hit me or storm out or possibly both, but when she yanks her phone out of her pocket, I nearly piss myself thinking her phone call is to Foster. That is until she speaks again...

"Finch, you are in so much damn trouble when I see you." She doesn't wait for a response before she hangs up and yanks me into her arms. "I'm sorry, Shay. How I could even think... You know what? It doesn't matter; I'm an asshole. Sorry."

I am so relieved I almost cry. The booze probably isn't helping my emotions, and her next declaration doesn't do much to help me rein them in. "I Promise we'll get to the bottom of this tomorrow. Let's change the sheets for tonight and possibly fumigate the damn mattress. No telling who the hell he had in here."

I fall asleep with thoughts of strangling Finch for scaring me. Confident Ness will do precisely what she promised. This, coupled with the alcohol, helps me sleep like a log until I feel something looming over me. My eyes flutter open only to discover Foss sitting in a chair next to my bed, and to say he looks pissed doesn't begin to cover it.

"Care to tell me what the hell is going on, Shay?"

Episode One Hundred Five:
Mistake

Foster

I KNEW NESSIE planned a girls' night with Shay, Maggie, and Sadie. It made me happy she did since it's something my girl has always wanted and never had. I even offered to purchase the wine for the festivities. The sheer number of bottles Ness loaded into the cart told me I wouldn't have the pleasure of Shay's company until sometime later today. I also figured all of them would be hung over this morning and need something to help soak up the rest of the booze. So I decided to bring them food.

I guess this was my first mistake. Coming into Shay's house without her inviting me. My second may have been believing she feels the same about me as I do about her. I suppose what I stumble on when I enter her room shouldn't surprise me, especially since she almost passed out when I told her I loved her.

Imagine my astonishment when I discover my cousin's scent permeating the room. I admit it shocked me when I realized the smell was heaviest on the sheets balled up on the floor in my mate's bedroom. Yet the surprise morphs into anger when I kick at the bedding and uncover a pair of his boxer shorts. My gut reaction was to wake her up, but logic won out. There has to be a rational excuse for this. So rather than confronting her when I'm this pissed off, I force myself not to give into my baser desire and instead impatiently wait for my mate to wake up.

But the second I see her eyes flutter, my tolerance is done.

"Care to tell me what the hell is going on, Shay?"

"Foster!" she yells as she scrambles out of bed. Luckily for my mate, I am not hungover. Otherwise, her face would have met the floor when her feet got tangled in the bedding.

"You should probably sit back down."

"Foss, I—we. Shit, I need a second," she tells me as she presses her hand to her forehead. Wine hangovers are the worst. It's all the damn sugar.

I may not understand what's happening, and regardless of how bad this looks, I don't want to watch her suffer. But my compassion and how I feel about this girl will only last so long, so as you can imagine, I have no intention of waiting all day for my answers. I hand her a bottle of water, some aspirin, and one of Nan's muffins she had packed for them.

"Thanks," she says as she lifts the bottle. I can't help but notice the slight tremble of her hand as she lifts the water to her mouth. This can be from either the amount of alcohol she consumed last night or, and this better not be the fucking answer, nerves from whatever I stumbled into.

When Shay flops back on her bed, throwing her arms over her eyes, my patience has come to an end, as has Shadow's, since the growl we give her is angrier than I intended. "Shay!"

"Ow," she winces at the abruptness of my reaction. "Can we talk later—"

"No."

As hard as I try to conceal my frustration, the second she peeks at me from under her arm, she realizes I am past the point of being put off.

"Foster..." Is that desperation seeping into her tone? Why? Why would my mate be worried? Her lack of response is doing nothing to calm me. In truth, it is pissing me off more. And this time, when Shadow growls, it snaps Ness awake too.

"Foster, what — what are you doing here?" Ness questions, and just like Shay, she instantly regrets her sudden movement. "Ohhhh, goddess, how much did we fucking drink last night?"

"All of it," I snap. "Now answer my fucking question."

"Nothing, Foster. Nothing happened. I don't know how...." Shay trails off, looking from me to Ness for help. But the instant I see her open her mouth to defend Shay, the look I give her silences her from continuing.

"That doesn't look like nothing," I advise, flipping my thumb toward the shit that shouldn't be at my mate's place.

"Foster—"

"Ness, this doesn't involve you."

"It does when you're acting like an ass."

"Vanessa, staying out of this would be in your best interest. In contrast, I'm still waiting for your answer, Shay."

"I said nothing happened."

"You classify me finding another man's underwear in your bedroom, even if it is my fucking cousin's, as nothing?"

Before the girls can say anything else, the shrill ring of Nessie's phone causes another groan from both women. But when Ness looks down at it, she quickly snatches it up.

"Can I call you back late—" the caller cuts her off. Their tolerance for these bullshit stall tactics is as limited as mine. She stumbles out of bed, trying to put some space between her and me. She did this hoping I wouldn't realize who was on the other end. Too late. I am already kicking the chair out from under me as I stalk in her direction.

"Give me the phone."

"I'm on a call, Foster," she snaps before lowering her voice and snarling, "and I said I would call you later."

Before she can hang up, I snatch the phone away from her. As much as she tries to convey anger, her eyes give away her fear. If Ness is afraid, it can only mean one thing. She believes something happened too.

"Finch—"

"Foss, what the hell is Ness's problem? She calls and leaves some cryptic fucking message on my phone that I'm in big trouble."

"Care to share why your scent is all over a set of sheets in Shay's room?"

"What? Bullshit—"

"Not just that, your fucking underwear too."

"Quit fucking around, Foss, and tell me what's happening."

"I'm not fucking around."

"Foster, you can't think I'm screwing around with Shay. I would never do anything to hurt you. You know better than that, man. You're my brother."

"Yeah, I know. Just be at Stooges in four hours." I don't wait for him to say anything else, opting to hang up. His cousin did not make this demand. It came from his Alpha, and the tone I delivered my request leaves no room for misinterpretation. I do know him, and he's right... he has never crossed that line, which only results in more questions than answers.

"You'll believe him, but not me?" Shay asks.

"He's never lied to me before." The look on her face couldn't have been any worse than if I had slapped her. I know why she withheld information when she first arrived here. She was afraid. I shouldn't have said this to her, especially since I didn't make her life easy when she arrived in Lake.

"That's a low blow, Foster. You can take your damn attitude and get the hell out of my house."

"That's all you have to say to me?"

"Until you stop throwing accusations at me. Yes!"

"Then we're done here," I snarl as I storm out of the house. I want answers, but right now, more than the answers, I need space to process this shit. And a drink to squash this burning rage. I turn to leave with my cousin hot on my heels.

"Foster," Ness yells.

"It would be best if you didn't put yourself in the middle of this, Vanessa."

I love my cousin, but this is one time she needs to mind her business, and if she doesn't, the next command will come from her Alpha.

Episode One-Hundred Six: Eff Off

Shay

*W*HAT IN THE hell just happened? How did a girl's night turn into this mess? I want to rewind the last twenty hours or so. Back to me lying in Foster's bed with his arms wrapped around me as we discussed our plans for the day. I don't know why Finch would do this to me, but I intend to find out.

For the first time, I contemplate calling off work to get to the bottom of this shit, but I dismiss it almost as fast, knowing I can't do something like this to Seamus. It's not his fault, and my calling off would only make this shitty situation his problem to contend with.

So the Finch issue will have to wait. When I climb into the shower to prepare for my shift at Stooges, I find my shampoo discarded on the shower floor rather than the shelf where I always put it. Don't tell me whoever Finn brought here took a damn shower and helped herself to my shit. I am so going to kick his ass when I see him.

I am no less irritated when I barge through the door at Stooges thirty minutes later. But seeing Hyde's smiling face sitting in his new favorite chair next to Jerry, I let some of my frustration melt away. I'm still ashamed of myself that because of my inability to refuse my mate, he felt he had to move his spot.

"Hey, kiddo, I didn't know you had the early shift today."

"Mandy told Seamus she couldn't work, so I told him I could cover both shifts since Beth is still learning the ropes." Seamus hired Beth, as he tells it, as my replacement when my Luna duties pull me away from the bar. It looks like this won't be happening anytime soon.

"So we get the pleasure of seeing," hiccup, "your smiling face all day?"

"Well, I don't know about the pleasure part, Jer, but I am here all day. Why are you two here so early?"

"Came in to watch the game," Hyde tells me.

"Where else would I be?" Jerry declares. It makes me sad knowing how lonely he is.

Thankfully, the bar is busy enough to help take my mind off everything, and by the time Ness comes in with Mandy and Sadie, I greet them with a smile.

"What time did you leave last night?" I asked Sadie since I noticed she wasn't on the loveseat any longer after Foster's early morning not-so-pleasant wake-up call.

"Oh–I umm… I—"

"How about you stop chatting with your friends and get your ass back to work." Riona. Of fucking course, this bitch would have to come in to make my already shitty day worse. Since I'm not in the mood to argue with her, I make a drink up and slam it in front of her before returning to the people I prefer talking to.

When Foster strolls into the bar two hours later, laughing with Atlas, I believe he may have figured out why Finn was in my house, but this thought swiftly disappears when he barely looks in my direction. Even more when he finds a table as far away from the bar and me as possible. And just like that, all the frustration and anger are back with a vengeance.

I'm pissed he could believe I would do something so terrible. I'm furious Finn put me in a position to feel like I had to defend myself, but the worst part is the fucking grin Riona is sporting, having witnessed his dismissal of me. If he didn't want to be around me, maybe he shouldn't have come into the one place he knew I would be... my workplace. And, of course, the bitch delighted in pointing it out.

"Oh my, is there trouble in paradise?"

"Is there something you want, Riona?"

"A refill to start. An Alpha to finish." I have to push Moon down as she growls and tries to drive forward. Now is not the time to shift and tear my boss's niece a new ass. Instead, I do what I am here to do...I start making her another drink, as Ness takes it upon herself to defend me in her typical crazy Nessie way.

"Keep dreaming, bitch."

"How do you know it's not his dream?"

"Because my cousin has taste, and what the hell is that smell? Oh, it's you. What are you wearing?" Ness asks as she takes a deep breath.

"My new favorite scent."

"What's that? Ode De Piece of Shit?"

Riona leans closer, dropping her voice but still ensuring she remains loud enough for me to hear her as her eyes settle on me. "No, it's called soon to be the Alpha's New Mate."

"Oh, so it's just called whore then?"

"Funny."

"I figured you, of all people, would appreciate it. Oh, and if you liked that, then you'll love this," Ness smiles sweetly before flicking her off.

"I look forward to the day you and the bitch behind the bar are kneeling in front of me as Foster announces me as the new Luna. Yeah, I'm talking about you, Shay."

Riona no sooner says this before she leaps from the bar stool to stroll over to the table Foster sits at while I try my best to keep Ness from knocking her on her ass. Nessie may be small in stature, but let me tell you, when I grabbed her arm as she threw a punch at Riona, she damn near yanked me across the bar.

"So, I have a question... Why is Ms. Big Tits over there talking to Foster like you don't exist? But more importantly, why does she smell like you, Shay?" Sadie asks as she shuffles up to the bar.

"I knew I recognized that scent!"

"Wait a minute, you said it stunk."

"On her, but not you."

"You called her a whore, Ness."

"Do you disagree?" When I stare at her, she sighs before saying in a rush. "Besides, I only said it to get under her skin. And she is over there with my stupid ass Alpha cousin because the dumbass bitch thinks she stands a chance with him." Ness yelled the last part loud enough to ensure Foster and Riona heard what she said.

131

No problem there since the entire bar... hell, the whole town heard her, and the ones present are currently staring at her like she lost her damn mind.

"What?" Ness's snapped response has several patrons turning to avoid eye contact. I get she hates Riona and thinks she's a vile bitch, but the rest of the bar didn't do anything, so she should chill out.

I know what I'm doing will most likely lead to more trouble. I can't help myself. Charging over to his table, I almost lose my mind when I find Riona running her finger up his arm as she whispers a private thought to him. The grin she gives me as she moves her chair closer to him has Moon growling. As pissed as my wolf is at Riona, I'm livid with him for allowing this to continue. Even Atlas seems shocked by the whole interaction.

"What the hell are you doing?" My eyes flick from him over to the bitch I am trying really damn hard not to hit.

"I'm not doing anything, Shay. Much like you didn't do anything. Right?" His eyes only meet mine when he asks the last part, but when I don't give him an immediate response, he turns his attention back to the bitch damn near bouncing in her chair about the entire situation. "Thought so."

"Is this how you want this shit to go, Foster?"

"Are you ready to tell me how the shit I found in your bedroom this morning got there?"

"I already told you I don't know."

"Then I guess this is how this shit is going to go." When he doesn't stop Riona from pushing her tits against his arm, I morph past irate to murderous. But I refuse to allow him to know how much it hurts me. My entire life, everyone has always expected me to just accept whatever anyone wants to heap on me. Unfortunately for Foster, I'm done letting people

132

treat me like a doormat. That goes double for the asshole who asked me to marry him a couple of days ago and then refused to believe me the first chance he got. Opting instead to turn his back on me, as everyone else has done throughout my life.

"Then I only have one thing to say to you. Don't fucking come around me ever again!" I direct the next part to the bitch whose grin just doubled in size. "He's all yours."

"Shay!" He yells when I spin to walk away from him.

"Fuck off, Foster." My response wasn't well received because I heard the chair slam against the floor when he came to his feet. I don't give a shit. I'm done... so fucking done with all of it. I need to get out of this bar and away from both of them before I do something I may regret.

"Beth, I have to go," I say before slamming open the door. I feel like shit leaving her here alone, but I can't stay. I understand if Seamus wants to fire me, but I'm sure he would prefer this to a homicide inside his bar. One that would force him to explain to his sister why her daughter was dead.

The second I round the back of the building, I yank my clothes off and release Moon. Since she can feel my pain, she doesn't insist we go back to figure out what the hell is happening. No, tonight she rushes away from the one person we always thought we would run toward. And with every mile we put between Foster, Shadow, and us, our heart breaks a little more.

Episode One-Hundred Seven: None of Your Business

Foster

"You JUST SCREWED up big time, Foster," Atlas interjects as he stands to block my path. We've been friends for a long time, and never... not once... have I ever wanted to hit him until now.

"I disagree. I think you made the right choice," Riona says as she wraps her arms around my neck.

"Let. Go!" I growl.

"Come on, Foss. You have to admit I'm a much better choice to be your Luna than some little wallflower who doesn't even have the courage to fight for her mate."

"Don't fucking say another word about Shay," I tell her through gritted teeth.

"You did this shit to yourself, Foss," Atlas says as he tosses twenty dollars on the table before he follows my mate out the door.

"We made progress toward what I know you've always wanted. Me." The woman I should never have allowed to touch me informs before kissing my cheek.

"No. We didn't." My snarled response while yanking her arms away from around my neck pissed her off. I don't care. I just hurt the only person I swore I would never do this to. The one person who means everything to me.

"Keep your grubby fucking hands off my cousin, before I rip them from your arms." Ness shrieks as she storms over from the bar.

She thinks she needs to defend me, but I can handle this chick alone. "I've got this, Nes—"

I don't have a chance to say the rest of her name before she slaps me. "And you're an asshole."

"Vanessa," I snarl.

"Don't you snarl at me and fuck you."

"Fuck me?"

"Yeah, fuck you, Foster. I have always thought you were the best man a girl could ask for. A man worth waiting for. So when I found out you and Shay were mates, I was over the goddamn moon knowing that after everything she had been through, you would make it your mission to erase all the awful shit and replace it with only good. But what do you do? You turn your back on her at your first opportunity to prove it. And worst yet, you rub this fucking pathetic she-wolf in her face. I'm ashamed of you, Foster."

"Ness, what in the hell would you think if you found something like this in Brady's room?"

"I get how bad it looks. Hell, I even questioned Shay about it myself last night, but unlike you, when she told me she didn't do anything, I believed her. Which is the same reaction I would have if my mate told me nothing fucking happened."

"Then why is his shit in her room?"

"Who the hell knows why Finn does any of the shit he does. If I had to venture a guess, he probably met someone here and decided driving back to pack land or to your place was too far, so he helped himself to Shay's empty house instead."

"Well, here's his opportunity to confirm this," I tell her, nodding toward Finn, who just came strolling through the door.

"Wait, this is about Finch?" Maggie and Sadie ask simultaneously as they come over to join us. I figured Maggie would defend him since they spend so much time together, but I didn't expect it from Sadie.

"I mean... I guess I thought Finn was with someone." Sadie continues.

When my eyes settle on Maggie, she's quick to respond. "Don't look at me. Finn and I are friends. Nothing more."

Finn's normal jovial attitude is nowhere to be found as his gaze settles on Ness. I already know Ness called and bitched at him last night. What I don't know is his side since she cut him off without letting him talk.

"Ness, do you want to tell me what your call was about last night?"

"Right after you tell us why your shit and stench are all through Shay's bedroom."

"Stench? You can say several things about me, Vanessa, but stink is not one of them."

"Have a seat, Finn," I say as I kick the chair out for him to sit down. While a part of me knows he isn't sleeping with my mate, another larger part is having a hard time working out why his shit was at her place.

His hesitation lasts only seconds before he yanks the chair further away from the table and drops heavily on it. His eyes never move away from mine as he waits for me to explain why this is still an issue.

"Explain why I found your shit in her room."

"I don't have any goddamn idea. I sure as shit didn't do it, and I can't imagine Shay did either."

"So it just magically appeared there?"

"No, Foster, I'm not fucking saying that. What I'm saying is someone is fucking with you and Shay, but it sure as shit isn't me. And the way she looks at you, it isn't Shay either. If you want to know, I suggest you look elsewhere."

"Where the hell have you been disappearing to lately?"

"If you have to know, I'm seeing someone."

"Really? Then why haven't I heard anything about it until now?" I ask.

"Because it's none of your business. Besides, she didn't want me to say anything."

"Why?" Ness demands as she slams her hands on her hips. Finn leans back in his chair, crossing his arms defiantly over his chest.

"Probably because she didn't want to get the fifth degree. Kind of like I am right now."

"Then you won't have any problem telling us who you've been screwing in Shay's bed."

"First, I never screwed anyone, Shay included, in Shay's bed. Second, who I'm seeing is none of your business."

"Finch, who were you with last night?" I ask. Ordinarily, I wouldn't care, but now I'm wondering if the girl he's seeing could be the one behind this. The more reluctant he is to confess who she is, the more I am left to believe it's Riona.

"Last night, I wasn't with anyone; however, I was with her all day yesterday and early this morning, and as much as it pains me to say this to you, Foster... I won't betray her trust, so I won't be answering your—"

"Me. Finch was with me." Sadie's admission is spoken so softly that I question if I heard her correctly or not.

"I asked him not to say anything because I know how much he is helping you, Maggie, and I didn't want you to think I was only doing it to hurt you. I know I did shit like this before, but I'm not like that anymore, and not when it comes to Finn."

"Sadie, I couldn't be happier for you or Finch. We're just friends. This won't change just because you two are dating."

"Never, Maggie," Finn confirms as he pats her hand.

"Not Riona?" I ask, knowing the answer even before he responds.

"Seriously, what kind of asshole do you think I am? That girl is nothing but trouble, not to mention the only guy she wants is you."

"And you never took Sadie to Shay's place?"

"Foster, I wouldn't do that to Shay."

"Neither would I," Sadie confirms.

"Fuck," I snap as I jump to my feet.

"Where are you going?" Finn asks as he takes Sadie's hand.

"To apologize to Shay."

"You better get down on your damn knees and beg her to forgive you, asshole," Ness snaps. She may have absolved me, but Shay is another story altogether. I can only pray to the goddess I haven't ruined everything.

Episode One-Hundred Eight: Top Shape

Max

*I*T'S BEEN FIVE weeks since I sent my scouts to Colorado, and I received word they just returned. Apparently, my brother knows they are back too, which is why Travis stormed into my office, making demands.

"They're here. Let's get the intel because it's time we make the trip back to Colorado," Travis says as he plops in the chair across from me.

I could lock the door to stop people from roaming in here while I'm getting my rocks off, and maybe if I cared about the chick, I would. The problem is, I don't give a shit about the ones who are so willing to drop to their knees. If I did, I certainly wouldn't send them on their way without reciprocating the favor. I have no issues with people finding a she-wolf on her knees in front of me. What I will never allow is anyone catching

Marcelle Valentine

me on my knees between some chick's legs. As much as I enjoy it, that shit makes you look weak.

"Why are you so hell-bent on this bitch? There is plenty of ass right here in Montana," I say as I push further back into the chair, giving the girl concealed under my desk more room to finish me off.

"Because she's the only bitch who has ever denied me, and if you haven't figured this out yet, brother. I. Hate. Being. Denied."

"Yeah, you've always been a whiny bitch." Natasha's tongue circling the head of my dick almost gives away what Travis is once again too damn oblivious to realize.

"Fuck you. I want her." Reaching down, I twist Natasha's hair in my hand and shove her harder down on my dick to ensure I spill every drop into her mouth. The only thing that mouth of hers is actually good for.

"What are you fucking doing over there?" Travis asks as he lifts himself from the chair. "Is that Erin?"

"Not this time," I advise glancing down at one pissed-off she-wolf whose eyes have narrowed to little more than slits. I imagine Tosh doesn't like the idea that she is not the only one I've had on their knees under my desk. Too bad. I have needs and a willingness to let anyone who offers their mouth a chance to fulfill them.

I have a room I can use for times like this, but I don't take whores into my bed. When I let a woman in my personal space, it's because they don't drop to their knees the second I ask them to. Something that doesn't ever happen lately.

"Alright, let's go. My brother and I have shit to discuss." I tell her as I flip my thumb to indicate she should vacate the space under the desk.

140

"I'm not dressed."

"It isn't anything my brother hasn't seen before. So chop-chop. Now."

"Tosh. Nice. That bitch knows how to use that fucking tongue." Travis says as he thrusts his hips up to mimic the act of fucking someone.

"You can't be serious," Natasha hisses.

"Do I look like I'm fucking joking?" When she doesn't move this time, I grab her arm and drag her out from under there. Am I worried she won't be back to service me again? Not at all. She's like a dog with a bone. Even if she doesn't come back, plenty of other women are around to fulfill my needs.

"What about me?"

"You have a hand and plenty of fucking toys. Use one." Natashia stomps over to her discarded shirt while Travis's mocking laugh serves no purpose other than to piss her off even further. "Oh, by the way, I'll probably need that again in a few hours. Why don't you send one of those sexy friends of yours next time?"

"Fuck you, Maximus."

"Hey Tosh, I'll be by in a little bit," Travis yells over his shoulder.

"Go to hell, Travis," she snarls as she slams the door behind her.

"Yeah, that's what I want from Shay. Her on her fucking knees, servicing me anytime I want it."

"It's more likely that wild cat would bite your dick off."

"Not if she doesn't have any teeth."

"You are one twisted bastard. You know that. Right, brother?"

"No more than you are. Brother." his hissed use of the word brother only proves how ridiculous he can be because if he thinks it bothers me, he's beyond fucking wrong. I press the intercom to tell the scouts I've kept waiting long enough while Tosh took care of my first and—in my opinion—most important priority; they can come in.

"Alpha," both men acknowledge as they enter my office. I got to say hearing that shit never gets old.

"Well?" Travis growls when his patience has reached its boiling point.

"Foster is the Alpha of the Ash Rock pack, and they do not use his sentinels in the same capacity as the previous Alpha utilized them. They actually patrol the grounds now."

"Doesn't surprise me. I figured this would be the first thing any Alpha worth a shit would change."

"He also has every wolf training no less than once a day. Other than his elite forces, who train twice. Once on their own, then once with him or some guys who aren't part of the pack."

"Atlas and Denver?"

"Yeah, I think that's their name."

"And what about Shay?" Travis couldn't care less what kind of shitstorm we are about to walk into as long as he can claim the chick who denied him. Fucking dumb little shit.

"She and Foster are together," this has a low growl rumbling deep in his chest. While I groan at his ignorance. Of course, she's with Foster, every fucking she-wolf, and half the human women surrounding Lake wanted him to claim them. It seems the only one who managed to accomplish it is the wolf my little brother wants.

The two scouts take a defensive step away, fearing what my brother might do. They don't have to worry too much because

I won't let him kill my two best scouts, no matter how pissed off he is. I imagine Kyle only blurts the next part because he hopes it will pacify my whiny little brother.

"But she still lives in the house owned by the old guy who owns the bar."

"You better be glad Seamus didn't hear you call him old."

"I'm not afraid of some old drunk Irish prick."

"That old drunk Irish prick could easily handle the two of you. So show the man some fucking respect." I may not care for how he sometimes acted with me, but he has more than earned the respect that these shifters standing in front of me will show him.

"You should know she only stays there when she works late or on nights Foster goes out on patrol."

"Wait, you mean to tell me the Alpha does patrol duty?" Trav asks.

"He does."

"That is too fucking hilarious for words. What a loser." Travis laughs. While Travis finds this funny, I'm not surprised by it. Foster is all about everyone pulling their weight, and what my dumb ass little brother doesn't understand is that it helps keep him in tip-top shape. I know I've lost much of my edge since the only thing I do anymore is sit around this damn pack house getting my cock sucked. While this does wonders for my mental health, it has tanked my physical attributes.

"So we can easily get to her then. We only have to wait for the wanna-be Alpha to go out for patrol. No problem." For Travis, it's all about claiming someone he has always wanted. For me, it's about taking something from the asshole I have always despised. I always avoided Foster when I was in top shape, which takes him from someone who would be difficult to deal with to someone we should both fear. Travis would do well to remember this. "When do we leave?"

"There is something else you should know."

"I think we're good," Travis snaps, but the glare I give him silences any further interruptions. There is a reason I sent my scouts to watch Foster's pack, and I will hear every bit of intel they have to give. I don't give a shit if Travis likes it or not.

"What else do you have?"

"The previous Alpha of this pack is with them."

"What? I surely heard you wrong. Because I killed him." I snarl.

"No, you didn't. Brady is alive, well, and is housed in his brother's pack."

Episode One-Hundred Nine: Pot Kettle

Shay

$\mathcal{J}$T'S BEEN TWO weeks since I stormed out of Stooges and told Riona she could have Foster. Since then, I will not accept any of his phone calls. I refuse to open the door when he shows up at my house. Ness, Finn, Brady, Maggie, and Sadie were all instructed not to call me on his behalf. I even talked Seamus into not letting him come to Stooges on the nights I work.

I think I have made it crystal fucking clear we're done.

Do I understand why he was initially upset? Yes, but what I will never comprehend is why he allowed Riona to behave the way she did, nor will I overlook it. Had he allowed me to explain without trying to get even for something I didn't do, we could have moved past this, but now none of it matters.

This time Moon isn't begging me to give him another chance. His reaction destroyed and hurt her as much as it did me.

The last thing I need to do is clear my shit out of his place and drop off the stuff he had at mine. Thankfully, Maggie's intel that the construction company owned by the pack has a big job they have to finish will allow me to put a period on this chapter of my shitty life. It gives me enough time to get in and out of his cottage without the fear of running into Foster.

With Ness offering to take me to his house, I have everything in place to finish this, and unlike her normal tardiness, today she arrived when I asked her to.

"Here's all your stuff from the packhouse," Ness says as she places the box on my couch.

"Thanks, Ness."

"Are you sure about this, Shay?" She asks as she taps the side of the box. "I know he acted like an asshole, and he has a shit ton of groveling to do—"

"Ness, this isn't about Foster begging. It's about me finally realizing I'm worthy of respect. Something Foster forgot," I tell her as I pick up his stuff.

"I suppose it doesn't matter that he realizes it now."

"Would it matter to you if Brady accused you of this shit?"

"I suppose not," she acknowledges, but I don't miss the dejected tone in her response. She wants Foster and me together. I get it. I'm sure if I asked Moon for her honest opinion, she would say the same thing, but I can't let go of how elated Riona was when she thought she won. I've had women look at me like that my entire life, but I never thought I would have to deal with it from my mate, especially after he confessed he wanted to spend the rest of his life with me.

He does, Shay. He not only confessed it... he declared it when he asked us to marry him. This is the first time she has asked me to forgive him.

Then he shit all over that declaration.

I'm not saying we should simply forgive him, but should we not hear him out? Remember, he thought we did what you are so upset about.

With Finn. He actually believed we could do something like that.

Would you have thought anything different if the roles were reversed? I'm not overly fond of it when she points out the obvious, but she's right. I would have thought the same thing. Where Foster and I differ is I wouldn't have let someone he hated hang all over me to prove a point.

He misses us.

And how do you know this?

Because Shadow told me.

How did you talk to Shadow?

While you were sleeping. It's the only time we can break through enough to hear each other.

We are not discussing this right now.

Does that mean we can talk about it later?

I'm not promising anything.

I'll accept that. With my wolf quiet again, I focus my attention out the car window.

"How long do you think you'll be?" Ness asks when we pull into his driveway.

"Aren't you coming in?"

"No, Shay. Foster is going to have a hard time understanding how I could bring you out here to collect your stuff. I don't want to hurt him further by helping you pack it."

"Not long," I promise. I can't be upset with her for not wanting to come in. He's her family... I'm nothing more than her

147

friend. For the first time since this shit began, I think about the sacrifices Finn and Ness have made for me.

Dropping the box containing his stuff on the table, I slowly search through each room to collect anything that belongs to me. After I walk out of here today, whatever I leave behind is gone for good.

Running my hand over the sofa, I can't help but remember all the memories we shared here. It's hard to remain mad with so many wonderful times repeatedly playing in my head. Before I realize what I'm doing, I pick up a shirt he haphazardly discarded on the couch and lift it to my nose. For the first time in weeks, I let his scent surround me.

The only thing this accomplishes is making me miss him more than I thought possible, as Moon whimpers her agreement. Faster than when I picked it up, I dropped his shirt and rushed into the bathroom on the main floor. I don't think I have anything in here; most of my stuff is upstairs in Foster's room and his bath.

"Shay." My heart stops. I don't have to turn around to know who is standing behind me. What I don't understand is why he's here. My eyes slowly lift to the mirror only to find him leaning against the door frame with his arms crossed over his bare chest.

The glistening sheen of sweat covering his torso tells me he was out for a run when I arrived at his house, or he shifted to let Shadow race here before I could leave when Nessie called to inform him of my whereabouts.

"I don't have anything to say to you, Foster." I groan as I toss the last of my shit into my bag.

"Really, because the time you spent with my shirt pressed against your face would say otherwise." Oh, for the love of the goddess, why did he have to see me do that? The better question is, why would I think it was a good idea?

Not knowing how to answer his question, I do the only thing I can think of; deflect his question with a comment of my own. "I put everything you left at my place in the box on the table."

"Shay, I don't give a shit about the stuff in that damn box. I care that I hurt you. I'm sorr—"

"Don't say you're sorry, Foster. I am so damn sick and tired of people telling me how sorry they are after they treat me like shit. Like this fucking word can erase the shit they said or did. Be man enough to admit you were mad, you wanted to hurt me, you accomplished what you set out to do, and leave it at that," I snap as I push past him to get my stuff from upstairs.

He grabs me from behind when I arrive at the top of the steps. His mouth presses to my ear as he tells me. "I was mad and hurt thinking about the possibility you would want someone else. I wanted you to hurt as much as I was. I am brave enough to admit I was wrong and willing to wait as long as you need to forgive me. I am sorry, Shay. I should never have let you walk out of Stooges believing I could ever want someone other than you. Please talk to me."

Taking a deep breath, I nod my head once. I will do for him what he wouldn't for me. Give him a chance to explain, but only after I finish getting my stuff because I don't know if hearing him out will change anything, and I don't want to have to stay one second longer than necessary if it doesn't.

"After I finish. I'll give you fifteen minutes."

"I'll take it," he says as he slowly releases his grip around my waist.

But everything changes the moment I walk into his room and discover her scent hanging heavy in the air.

Spinning to face him, I snarl, "I can't believe how fucking dumb I am."

"What are you talking about?"

"How long after I left the bar that night did it take you before you brought her here?"

"Brought who here?"

"Riona," I growl as I shove him away from me.

"She's never been here before."

"Really?" I snarl as I storm over to the source of the smell. Yanking the sheet from his bed, I toss it at him before saying, "Then how is her fucking scent all over your bed?"

"I don't know, but I can promise you I intend to find—"

"Bullshit!"

"Shay, I haven't been here since the last time we were here. Please believe me."

"Like you believed me!"

"I deserve that."

"I'll tell you what I don't deserve. Being forced to watch Riona rub her tits all over you. If you were okay with that, I don't think you would have any problem fucking her. We're done."

"Shay," he pleads as he grabs my arm to stop me.

"Let. Me. Go." I figured he would refuse, but to my surprise, he immediately dropped his hands. I waste no time storming out of his room, no longer caring about any of the shit I'm leaving behind. By the time I reach the bottom of the stairs, I'm running because the last thing I want to give him is my tears, and right now, they are blurring my vision and threatening to spill down my cheeks.

"Shay," Foster yells as he busts through his door as I climb into Ness's car.

"Shay?" she asks as she looks from her cousin to me.

150

"Please, Ness, don't ask questions. I need you to drive," I beg. She must take pity on me since she shifts her car into reverse as he runs up to the passenger door. When my gaze moves up to his, the first tear trickles over, making him falter long enough for Ness to pull away.

"Shay." His howls are the last thing I hear, which is heartbreaking since they are like a knife cutting away a piece of my soul.

Episode One-Hundred Ten: Honor

Foster

FOR THE FIRST time ever, I wish I had a male in my life as I was growing up. Maybe if I had, he could have taught me how not to fuck things up so colossally with my mate. As much as I want to see her and try to make things right, I don't. I won't because I want to honor her request and stay away.

After discovering Riona's scent all over my bed, it didn't take me long to figure out what had happened. She set this shit up, hoping it would drive a wedge between Shay and me. Which she only accomplished because I'm a damn idiot.

After I had put everything together, I tried calling Shay, but she refused to answer. I left her messages, but Sadie informed me she deleted them without listening. When I tried to see her at Stooges, Seamus told me she was taking some time off work before forbidding me from going to the place he rented to her. My last option was to tell Ness what I had discovered, only to have my heart pulled from my chest when she told me Shay already knew, and it didn't change anything.

I'm. A. Fucking. Idiot.

I would do anything to rewind time to that day because I assure you I would handle the entire situation differently.

As much as I want to ask our friends and family about her, I don't want them to feel like they have to choose. So I don't. Finn and Brady provide me with minor details, but the girls refuse to even say her name in front of me.

I always told you to let me do the talking, you blue-balled prick. And, of course, Shadow is beyond pissed at me.

I didn't hear you speaking up that day.

You didn't hear shit beyond the sound of your own voice, asshole. I knew she didn't do anything, or did you forget I have a connection with Moon? And unlike you, I believed my mate when she confessed nothing happened.

I know. I growl. Although Shadow has every right to be as mad at me as Shay is. He lost his mate because of my stupid ass too.

I didn't lose shit. Moon still loves me, but I will tell you one thing: you better figure out how to fix this shit. Because if you think I will spend the rest of my life with the only connection to my mate being our mind link when your fucking ass is sleeping, you've got another thing coming. Figure this out, or I will.

You will what?

Figure out how to be with my mate without you interfering. If I have to be Shay's loyal hound during the day and Moon's mate at night... so be it.

You could only do that if we never shifted back.

Exactly. So unless you want to walk around on all fours for the rest of your damn life, Foster. I suggest you figure this shit out now.

Shay doesn't want to—

I don't want to hear your excuses. The only thing I want is for you to fix this shit, blue-balls.

He's right. I need to figure out how to fix this shit.

You got one thing right. Shadow interjects.

What's that?

You are a fucking idiot.

Thanks. But he's already tuned me back out. If nothing else, I need to figure out how to let Shadow see Moon before he does something stupid or starts howling nonstop, which will drive me fucking insane.

*****

Shay

I'm surprised Foster has honored my request and left me alone. I know Moon and Shadow talk, which they can only do because of our proximity to the pack. If I suddenly picked up and moved across the country, their link would be severed. Not that I plan on doing this to either one of them. They didn't do anything wrong, and as long as Shadow keeps his promise to leave Foster in the dark about my life, I'm fine with them keeping their bond.

Seamus has thankfully allowed me to take on some of his administrative duties, like the books, purchasing supplies, and making the schedule. Which will enable me to work from home. I can't do this forever, but for now, it gives me the space I think we need and grants Foster and me the time to move past our breakup.

I have also limited my time with Ness, Maggie, and Sadie. It is hard for them to stay loyal to their Alpha since Maggie and Sadie officially joined Ash Rock when hanging out with me all the time. Their first priority must be the pack... as it should be. Foster hasn't demanded they tell him what I'm doing, even though he would be well within his rights as their Alpha. I think he understands it would only drive a wedge further between us if he did.

After finishing everything for Seamus, grabbing something small for supper, and throwing on some pajama pants, I decided to watch a movie. It's nothing I really want to watch, but it helps me keep my mind off him.

I'm twenty minutes into the show when Moon's whimpers, and her nervous energy, have me taking notice.

When you have an anxious wolf inside you, it's like having a pet who paces nonstop from window to door. When she refuses to calm down, I am left with few options other than investigating why she is so restless. It only took me a second to discover the culprit.

Furious that he is ignoring my request. I yank open the door and snarl, "Go home, Foster."

While it may not be Foster's form sitting on the porch, I know he's in there. I also understand how hard this has been on Shadow and Moon, and seeing Shadow waiting patiently out on the porch, I despise being mean to him.

Please, Shay. Please don't send him away.

I don't want to talk to Foster.

Shadow promises Foster won't say anything to you.

Moon.

Please, Shay, let me spend some time with my mate. If Foster doesn't honor his promise, we'll come straight home, and I'll never ask for this again. Telling her no is hard enough, but I know I lost this battle when Shadow moves closer to nuzzle my hand.

"You tell Foster he is not to speak to me through our mind link. I'm doing this for Moon and you and only you two. If he promises to abide by my terms, you can spend some time with Moon," I tell Shadow. Since I can't hear Shadow's thoughts, I must wait for him to relay Foster's response to Moon, who will then tell me.

He agreed. Moon squeals. Her sheer delight is evident in her response.

I'm amazed that after two hours of letting Moon and Shadow romp through the woods together, Foster kept his word and said nothing to me. I heard him laugh once when Shadow tried to impress Moon and fell into the creek, but nothing else. I am not ashamed to admit hearing him laugh after all this time was like medicine to my shattered soul.

Like the first time Foster and I released our wolves to run together, they chase each other, wrestle, and lay side by side when they rest. I can't tell you how happy I am seeing how much Moon has changed and grown since that day. It seems so long ago, back to a time when she didn't have a name, didn't understand how to play when Shadow tried, and now she's like a normal wolf.

Everything is perfect until Shadow dives on top of Moon, and Foster takes advantage of me being pinned under his frame.

Faster than Shadow can stop him, Foster returns to his human form. And as hard as Moon struggles to break his hold on us, he's stronger than we are.

"Shay, please don't blame Shadow for this. He's fighting to take back control. So I'm asking you not to punish Shadow for me breaking my word."

"I know I made you a promise, Shay, and I fully intended on honoring it but hearing you laughing and being this close, I knew I may never get another chance."

Moon whimpers as she struggles to get out from under his enormous frame.

"I'm sorry I hurt you. I would do anything to make this right. I'm an idiot because I let down the only person in this world I love with every piece of my soul and each part of my heart." My breath shudders, hearing him say this to me after all this time.

"I promise I won't bother you anymore. You can go back to work; I won't come in. You can spend time with Ness, Maggie, Sadie, Finn, and Brady; I won't interfere. The pack is still here for you if you ever need anything. If you allow Shadow access to Moon, I promise I'll never force the shift again. He tried to stop me, but I overpowered him."

Moon's whimpering cries reinforce her fears of me refusing to allow this to happen again. I've lost my mate, and now because he didn't uphold his promise, she's terrified she is losing hers.

"You deserve better than what I did to you," he runs his thumb against Moon's cheek. "Riona could never take your place. You will never understand how deeply I regret letting her think she could or using her to make you jealous."

He leans closer to Moon's face. "I miss you, I miss us, but I'm ready to let you go so you can find whatever will make you happy. I love you, Shay, and I always will."

He kisses the side of Moon's head before he pushes off of us, and before we regain our footing, Foster is gone, Shadow is back, and my heart hurts more now than it did the day Ness left him standing outside his cottage.

This is not the first time since everything happened that I realized how much I've missed his touch. So why can't I tell him as much?

Episode One-Hundred Eleven: Experience

Foster

I KEPT MY promise to her after the night in the woods and haven't bothered Shay. She has graciously allowed Shadow to continue seeing Moon, and while it's difficult being so close to her without being able to talk to her, I do it for our wolves. They have been through enough shit in their lives; they deserve a little happiness now.

The worst part is hearing her laugh because of something stupid Shadow did. It's both like a balm to soothe the parts of me missing her since she left and torture knowing it is only because I was too pigheaded to listen that I lost her.

Tonight will be the first time in weeks I plan on going into Stooges for the tournament. I'm not sure if it's darts or pool tonight. I'm not in the mood for any of it, but I promised Finn I would be there after Ness confirmed Shay isn't scheduled to work.

As much as I dread the whole night, Ness can't contain her excitement. Today is the first time Ness and Brady are going out since they made everything official. When Finn told her he planned on bringing Sadie, Ness mistakenly called it a group date night until I reminded her I'm single, and so is Maggie. Her sympathetic look doesn't take away the sting of knowing I'm the reason for this.

"What time do you want to head over to Stooges?" Finn asks as he strolls into my office with Brady.

"Ness is positive Shay isn't going to be there?"

"She said Seamus gave her the night off because the best way for Beth to learn how to deal with a tourney night was to jump in with both feet."

"I should probably stay here and get a work—"

"Don't say get a workout in, Foss, because you work out more than any other wolf in this damn pack. You don't need a workout. You need to get your ass out of here; stop torturing yourself about Shay and have a damn beer with your favorite cousin."

"Ness did say she would be there."

"Up yours, asshole. But I'll take it even if Nessie is the only reason you're going."

"Alright, let me finish up a few things here, then we'll head over to Stooges."

Two hours later, everyone is packed into my truck. I'm not sure how I got roped into being the designated driver tonight, but Finn's unwillingness to let me stay home is all beginning to make sense now. But it's frustrating because if anyone needs a night of getting shitfaced, it's me.

It's strange walking into the bar that has been like my second home after so long, and even though everyone assured me she wouldn't be here tonight, I can't help but look toward the bar, hoping to find her there. Who I see is Mandy, the new girl Beth and the chick who ruined my life, Riona.

"Hi, Foss," Mandy says with a little wave. I give a cursory wave to Mandy while ignoring Riona and the damn beaming grin she gives me before I make my way over to the table Ness has already commandeered for our group.

"So we're all signed up for the tournament," Ness announces with a fist bump. "And I totally plan on kicking all of your asses."

"Never going to happen, babe," Brady tells her as he kisses the top of her head.

"Yeah, 'cause I'm taking the win home tonight," Finn declares as he pulls Sadie onto his lap.

"I'll just be happy if I hit the damn target," Maggie laughs.

"It's called a board, not a target," Ness corrects. Ever since Finn and I taught her and Lindsey how to play, Nessie thinks she is a pro.

"Well, if you ask me, you are all wrong. My money's on Foster," Riona says as she leans against my chair. The only reason I haven't torn her a new ass is because of Seamus. Just as I prepare to shove her off me and tell her to stay the fuck away, Ness beats me to it.

"Get your ass away from our table."

"Your Alpha doesn't seem to mind."

"Whore," Ness doesn't seem to mind that she is attracting the attention of everyone around us, but then again... neither does Riona.

This dumb chick can't take a hint, so I guess I'll have to be more direct. Which results in me pulling away from Seamus's niece. Repeatedly saying this helps remind me who her uncle is. The fact I love the guy is her only saving grace. I am getting ready to tell her to stay the fuck away from me when she gives me a quick peck on the cheek, which only serves to piss Ness off further and makes me regret I haven't had a conversation with her sooner. One in which I tell her if she comes around me again, she will regret her decision.

"I'll be rooting for you from right over there," Riona murmurs, and if the look Ness gives her is any clue, I would have to say Riona's focus is on my cousin.

"I see you still haven't lost your touch," Atlas laughs as he pulls a chair over to the table.

"Shut up, asshole. Didn't know you were coming tonight."

"I wasn't planning on it, but... Listen, Foster, I need to tell you something."

"Okay."

"I brought someone with me."

"No shit. Where is she?"

He clears his throat and shifts slightly, and the instant I see who's standing at the door with Denver, rage races through me as I growl. "Shay? You fucking brought Shay with you?"

*****

Shay

When Finch and Ness kept asking me if I had to work tonight, it didn't take long to figure out they wanted to know if Foster could go into Stooges. So rather than picking up the shift, I passed it off to Beth and put some distance between the bar and me.

I figured this would be best because the more time I let Moon spend with Shadow, the more I want to talk to him. You cannot know how difficult it is to be in the same vicinity as someone you love and never say a word to them. Especially after what Foster and I had.

This is how I found myself outside a bar owned by none other than Atlas. I admit it shocked me when he pulled up on his bike. I can't explain how he knew the wolf was me, but he did. With no hesitation, he strides directly over to where I am standing.

"Hey Shay, what are you doing over this way?"

Since I could not answer him, my response was to tilt my head. I've said it before, and I'll say it again. This man may not be a shifter, but he is definitely not normal.

"Right. Do you want to come in for a drink?" I would, but unless he plans to serve me my drink in a dish Moon can lap it from, it won't happen because the second I shift back, I'll be standing in front of him without a stitch of clothes on. Which is not going to happen.

He must sense why I'm wavering because a booming laugh erupts from him before he tells me, "I've got something you can put on."

I don't know why I trust him as much as I do, but there has always been something about him and Denver that has put me at ease. After I put on the jeans and t-shirt he provided, I joined him out at the bar.

"So now you want to tell me what you're doing over this way?"

"Just out for a run."

"Uh-huh, and that run wouldn't have anything to do with a certain Alpha at Stooges right now?"

"No, not at all," I lie before taking a gulp of the drink I found waiting for me when I came out. This shit is stronger than I'm used to, and I cough like I've never had a drink before right now.

"Smooth," I choke. This causes Atlas to laugh at me again.

"Well, who is this pretty lady?" A woman in her fifties asks as she strolls behind the bar.

"Name's Shay," I say as I stick my hand out.

"And manners. I'm impressed, Atlas. She's not like the other girls you all normally bring around here. I'm Madge."

This is like the good gossip you never get. A peek into Atlas's life, and I admit I'm intrigued. "And what kind of girls do you normally bring around here?"

"First, Madge, I don't bring girls to the club. Second, Shay already has a man in her life."

"Uh," I try to interject, only to be cut off by Madge.

"Really? So who's the lucky man to land such a beautiful girl?"

"No one." "Foster." Atlas and I say simultaneously.

"Nice. He's quite the catch. Like this one over here," Madge says as she flicks her thumb in Atlas's direction. Which causes him to shake his head but with a grin covering his face.

"Well, if I'm being honest, Foster and I aren't together any longer."

"Oh, sweetie, I'm sorry. He's such a nice young man."

"He is a great guy, but sometimes things just don't work out."

"Do you mind me asking what happened?"

"Misunderstanding."

"Wait. So you're telling me a misunderstanding is the only thing keeping you away from a man you called great?"

"A big misunderstanding?" I say questioningly because my response sounds ridiculous when you put it as she did.

"Oh. So, you cheated on him, or he cheated on you, kind of misunderstanding?"

"No."

"Since I know Foster well enough, I know he didn't hit you."

"Absolutely not," I reply quickly, shocked anyone could even think something like this about Foster.

"And you didn't hit him?"

"No." This time I answer with a chuckle, thinking about the times I challenged him in the sparring ring and how easily he took control of the situation.

"Did he lie?"

"No."

"Did you lie?"

"No."

"Then, sweetheart, I got to be honest. I'm not seeing the disconnect here."

"It's hard to explain."

"It normally is," she says while nodding her head. "Can I give you a piece of advice?"

"Yeah," I like her. She is a no-bullshit kind of woman with a kind face. It's refreshing.

"If you can't give voice to what he did, or you did wrong, then it's not worth worrying about, and in my experience, anything not worth worrying about is not worth losing someone you so obviously care for." She gives me one last smile before she steps back with her arms crossed.

"Atlas?" I may be talking to Atlas, but I can't stop grinning at Madge.

"You ready to go to Stooges?" Atlas asks, and I don't miss the amusement thick in his voice.

"We're going to Stooges. Hot damn, I think the tourney is going on tonight," Denver says as he strides into the room.

"I don't know. Are we, Shay?"

The only answer I have to give him is a smile.

Episode One-Hundred Twelve: Round Two

Shay

I CAN TELL you the second we walked into the bar, Hyde, Jerry, and Beth looked relieved. Mandy looked pissed, and the bitch Riona looked entirely too comfortable slung over Foster's shoulder. Which led me to believe I had made a huge mistake coming here.

"Don't rush off just yet. Look at him, Shay. I mean, really look at him. He doesn't want her over there." Atlas says softly as he gently grasps my arm to stop me from turning to bolt straight back out the door we just walked through.

The exhale I release does little to help my frazzled nerves. I'm unsure what I hoped would happen here tonight, but I know I don't want things to continue as they have been for the last two months.

"Do you want to come over with me?"

Marcelle Valentine

"What if he doesn't want me over there?" I ask while biting my lower lip.

"Shay, this is Foster we're talking about; of course, he wants to talk to you," Atlas declares in his straightforward, no-nonsense tone while he looks down at me. He answers his own question for me when I don't respond or move to follow him. "I'll tell you what, let me talk to him, and you can come over to join us when you're ready or for as long as I can keep his ass over there once he realizes you're here."

When I nod, he doesn't waste any further time as he strides over to the table they are sitting at just as Riona spins to walk back up to the bar. The look covering her face resembles a fat cat after enjoying a bowl of cream. This is until she discovers me standing here. The look she gives me informs me she is about as happy to see me here as Mandy is, maybe less. But almost as fast, she shifts her expression back to gloating. A look that causes both rage and a sense of inferiority to settle in my stance.

Maybe she got what she wanted, and Foster decided she would be the better option. It's been over a month since I saw him, and I flat-out refused to let anyone tell me anything about him, so it's entirely possible they're together. This thought results in my shoulders slumping as the hope I felt leaving Atlas's club fades away.

"Don't you let that chick bother you," Denver murmurs.

"How can I not? Something is happening between them; otherwise, Foster wouldn't have sat there letting her wrap her arms around him. Really, I can't blame him."

"Shay, every couple has disagreements."

"I'm not only talking about our fight."

"I'm not following."

"I'm talking about Riona. All you have to do is look at her. She's stunning."

"She's pretty with a vile soul, so she doesn't hold a candle to you, Shay, so stop fretting over it," Denver tells me as he leans beside my ear. My heart leaps out of my chest when Foster whips around to face us.

"Oh fuck," I say, once again doubting my decision to come here as I back closer to Denver.

"Just wait," I do what Denver says and continue watching while Atlas puts a hand on his shoulder. Foster looks from him to me a few times before he rubs the back of his neck. I almost stumble over Denver's feet when Foster stands up.

"I'll be over at the bar if you need me," Denver whispers before he's gone, and I come face to face with the man I have wanted to talk to for weeks but didn't know how to.

"Sorry, Shay, Ness said you wouldn't be here. I'll head out."

Madge's advice seems to play on repeat, and I know she's right. Am I really going to let a few words said in the heat of the moment stop me from having him in my life? Even if our relationship doesn't return to what it was before, I know I want him here in some capacity. I find the courage to stop him before he can walk past me and out of my life again.

"Wait. You don't have to go," I softly say, placing my hand on his arm. When his eyes drop to the point of contact, I pull my hand back. Shit, I shouldn't have done that because I know from experience that he doesn't want other women touching him when he is with someone.

"Sorry," I mutter as I drop my gaze from his.

"For what?" he asks as he tilts his head, trying to capture my attention again.

"I shouldn't have done that," I flick my fingers toward the spot on his arm I was touching, "with Riona watching."

"What the fuck does she have to do with you touching me?"

As much as I want to be happy for him, I can't help the pang of jealousy coursing through me. Especially since I know Riona is the entire reason we broke up to begin with. I have never wanted to hit someone as much as I want to punch her... but I won't. I keep my hands and sarcastic words to myself for Seamus as much as Foster's sake. Thankfully, he drops the whole Riona conversation in favor of another one I don't want to have.

"I thought you didn't want anything to do with me?"

I exhale, knowing that, unlike the Riona topic, he will not be so willing to let this one go. Besides, isn't this what I came here for? "I was mad at you, but if I'm being honest, I think I was more hurt by the entire interaction, which I imagine is how you felt when you found his stuff in my room."

"I should have given you a chance to explain. There was no way you would have done something like that, and I know it. I'm sorry."

"You don't owe me an apology, Foster."

"Yes. I do," he says, pushing my hair out of my face before resting his hand against my cheek. It feels nice... actually better than nice to hear him acknowledge his mistake, but it's the contact I like most.

"So, can we go somewhere to talk?"

"How about we start with a drink? My treat, and then see where it goes from there." The smile he gives me confirms he agrees with my plan.

"Get your ass over here, Foss," Ed, the mill supervisor and tournament arranger extraordinaire, hollers.

When Foster hesitates, I nod in Ed's direction, indicating he should go, "Raincheck on the drink."

"Wanna join the tournament? I think we can find a spot for you." His confident tone may convey one emotion, but his eyes say he hopes I'll say yes.

"Nah, I'm a one-and-done kind of girl."

"I see, so you win once, and now you won't give me a chance to win the title back?"

"Now you're getting it," I laugh as I push him toward the crowd waiting for him to join them.

He walks away several feet before spinning to look at me again. "You're not leaving, right?"

"Nope, I'm going to drink with my two favorite bar patrons."

"I thought I was your favorite?" When the only answer I give him is a half-smile, he throws his hands over his heart while he continues to back toward the impatiently waiting Ed. "You're killing me, beautiful."

Hearing him call me beautiful after such a long time releases a surge of emotions I haven't felt since the day I walked away from him. The kind that flutters through your belly and lands right in your core. When he turns away from me, it hits me how much I've missed talking to him.

"Oh, and Foster."

He doesn't seem to care about making them wait, even as Ed and several others groan when he turns his attention back to me. "Good luck."

"Suddenly, fortune seems to be shining on me," he declares with a wink.

Hyde and Jerry welcome me in their typical response, which means they enthusiastically yell my name while drawing it out. Twenty minutes into the tournament, Atlas comes to where I'm sitting to ask if I'll be okay. I guess something came up, so he and Denver have to leave. He's a great guy. If I had told him I didn't want to stay, Atlas would have taken me anywhere I wanted to go, including right back to his clubhouse, so I could continue chatting with Madge.

When I assure him I'll be fine, he leans over to give me some sage advice. Advice about Riona, Foster, and me. I suppose it won't surprise anyone that he favors Foster and me getting back together.

Riona, on the other hand, has been giving me the evil eye all night long. Before he leaves, he says something to Finch, who looks over at me with a grin before he claps Atlas on his back and agrees with whatever Atlas says.

Foster is winning rounds like his life depends on it. I don't miss his gaze focused on me anytime he's not throwing. When he gets to the final match, the entire bar goes crazy when he wins it in nine throws, me included. But he silences me when his heated gaze falls on me. Warmth spreads across my face and chest before traveling to the spot I want him to touch. If half the town wasn't in the bar tonight, I would tell him about the panties I have on, knowing he would strip me of them without a second thought.

My eyes move from the man watching me to the table he so skillfully bent me over the night he discovered the lace thong. Thoughts of him taking me from behind while his thumb circled my clit play out in vivid detail. Never in my life have I wanted to relive a memory as much as I do this one.

He doesn't miss where my focus is or how I squirm in my seat as I squeeze my thighs together. My heart hammers in my chest as I watch him stalk in my direction, but every dirty thought he produces fades to fury when Riona runs over and smashes her lips against his.

Without thinking about the ramifications, I storm over and yank her away from him before I smash my fist into the lips, still swollen from the aggressive kiss she gave him.

"Don't fucking kiss my mate," I snarl. I'm not sure who's more surprised by my actions: Seamus, the bar patrons, the bitch who fucked everything up, our friends, me, or Foster. His shock melts away as he pulls me into his arms.

"Your mate?"

"Um... well... if—"

He doesn't give me a chance to finish before his mouth is on mine as he claims my lips the way she had hoped to do with his.

Episode One-Hundred Thirteen: Humiliated

Shay

*A*S MUCH AS I fantasized about Foster taking me in the middle of the bar, discretion won out as I decided the better course of action was to get him out of there before he discovered what I was wearing under my jeans.

Foster insisted on taking me home even though I probably could have walked there faster than getting in his truck and driving. I imagine he took his time because he wanted to spend as much time with me as possible. Which is something I don't have any issues with.

When he finally pulls into my driveway, our days and months apart feel like a distant nightmare. One I hope we never have to relive again.

"Would you like to come over to my house tomorrow? We could let Shadow and Moon get some exercise, then I'll make us some dinner."

"Yeah, I think I'd like that."

He walks me to my door and hands me the keys to his truck. I admit I'm confused. I guess my non-poker face gives it away when he laughs.

"So you can come to my house whenever you're ready tomorrow. Without having to depend on Nessie to come to pick you up."

"You could always get me."

"Shay, if I had it my way, you'd be coming back with me tonight, but I'm willing to wait."

"How are you getting home then?"

"I'll shift."

"Foster, that's silly. Take your truck."

"I could use..." he clears his throat while he rubs the back of his neck. "The distraction from what I would rather be doing."

I give him an innocent kiss before slipping into my house, knowing I am seconds away from saying fuck it and attacking him on my front porch. The logical part of me knows Foster is right; we need to talk about what happened and not just fall into bed together, but the ache building inside me is arguing in favor of the falling idea.

"Sleep well, beautiful," Foster quietly says from the other side of the thin slab of wood, keeping me from him.

Sleep well? Sleep well? How in the hell does he expect me to sleep when the only thing I can think about is him removing my clothes, preferably while he's completely nude. When lust wins out over logic, I yank the door open, but he's already gone, leaving me to wonder if it's too early to go over to his house.

"Goddess, Shay, get it together and stop acting like a horny teenager," I scold myself as I wander into my bedroom. My bed immediately brings thoughts of him buried between my thighs, which causes another round of aching right where I fantasize he's kissing. This is going to be one hell of a long night.

****

As suspected, I tossed and turned all night long. When the first rays of the sun filtered through my curtains, I gave up and got out of bed. As much as I wanted to drive straight to the one place where I knew I would find him, I forced myself to stay home.

While sitting at the kitchen table having a second cup of coffee and contemplating what time would be considered acceptable to show up at his cottage, my phone alerts me to a new message.

My heart rate accelerates when I flip it over and see his name on the screen. Without delay, I open the text to find a picture taken outside his house of the woods beyond with six words: *Morning, beautiful. We're awaiting your arrival.*

I'm running for the door before my response goes through to his phone: *See u soon.*

I don't know why I want to appear so unaffected by all this, but I do. This is why when I turn onto the dirt road I know will take me to him, I slow the truck down to the actual speed limit rather than the eighty I drove the rest of the trip. When I pull to a stop at his house, I find Foster leaning against a fence post, peeling the bark from a stick he's holding. I know this is a shitty thing to be happy about, but it appears he didn't get any more sleep than I did last night.

"Morning, beautiful."

"Morning, Foss."

"Sorry for texting so early, but Shadow was anxious to start our day."

Moon laughs before telling me. *Shadow said he admits to being damn anxious, but not to let him fool you because blue balls couldn't even sleep last night thinking about us coming here today.*

Blue balls?

Shadow's nickname for Foster. This causes another round of laughing from Moon while I grin at Foster.

"Just Shadow?"

"Well, I may have been slightly impatient."

Shadow said, slightly impatient his ass. He had to make Foster go back inside seven times last night when he decided they were done waiting.

Tell him next time... don't. My comment causes another round of laughter from Moon while my eyes move up to meet his.

"Only slightly, blue balls?"

"Shadow!" Foster growls, before he begins what I imagine is a heated conversation between his wolf and him.

It appears Shadow won out when he exhales loudly before grumbling, "Okay, maybe more than slightly."

Walking further into the woods, I strip, and just before I shift to allow Moon her time with Shadow, I tell him, "Next time, don't let Shadow stop you."

I don't miss his low groan as Moon sprints away from our exasperated mate and toward our favorite spot. The place she received her name. We romp through the woods all day, letting Shadow and Moon play. Even though Foster and I ensured they had time together when we weren't, they were always concerned I would take it away from them. And even though Foster and I don't talk to one another much, it's not like it was before. If anything, I would say it's because we are both more than a little sexually frustrated.

I am so wrapped up in Shadow and Moon's enjoyment that it is not until Foster asks if I am hungry that I realize how late it has gotten. When we arrive at his house, Foster has no problem shifting back to his human form, and oh... my... goddess... what a form it is. While I hesitate. It's not like Foster hasn't already seen every inch of me up close and personal; it doesn't matter because I am still getting used to shifting around someone else.

He understands me better than most, so he opens the door and jerks his head toward the interior, indicating I don't have to shift back before I go in. Needing a second to myself, I race upstairs, and only when I am alone in his room do I shift back. With my back against his door, I concentrate on regaining control of my ragged breath. Why did he have to show me what I had missed all these months?

With his perfect frame refusing to vacate my every thought, the ache I had last night for him turns into a full-blown fire. There is absolutely no way in hell I will be able to sit through an entire meal with the throbbing currently taking up residence at my core.

"You have to do something, Shay. Think. Think."

A quick look around his room reveals one possibility: a cold shower. This will work since the cold will take care of the heat, and the water should squash the fire. Without another thought, I climb into his shower. The problem is the only thing it does is make me shiver. I still want Foster every bit as much as I did when I scrambled in here.

Fuck. My. Life.

Back in Foster's room, I frantically look for anything else to help me, especially when he yells that dinner will be ready in five minutes. Shit, how long have I been up here?

Okay, suppose I want to make it through dinner without my legs squeezed together while thoughts of him screwing me on his dinner table tease me repeatedly the entire time. What choice do I have? I'll tell you none. In that case, I realize the only option is to relieve some of the tension he is responsible for.

"I need a few more minutes, then I'll be down," I yell after I crack the door open just enough so he can hear my response.

"Okay."

With his confirmation, I creep over to his bed and pull the sheets back. I know it's disgraceful to pleasure myself in his bed while the man waits for me downstairs, but I don't see any other option here. I climb between the sheets because I know I'll find his scent there, and I'm hoping it will help speed this process along.

As I suspect his woodsy aroma fills my nostrils, overtaking my senses, the shame of what I'm doing slips away as I slide my hand down my body to massage the throbbing he's responsible for. With one hand circling my clit, the other finds my sensitive nipples waiting to be teased.

When I roll my head to press my face against his pillow, the smell moves me past horny to ready to explode. Inhaling deeply, I slide two fingers inside to increase my pleasure. To keep the friction where I need it most, I press the palm of my hand against my clit. Thankfully, the moan that escapes me is muffled by the pillow I have my face against.

"Shay." Foster's voice as he enters his room is beyond mortifying. For the love of the goddess, did he have to come in and catch me masturbating in his damn bed? I yank my hand away from my soaking-wet core as I pull his sheet over me.

"NO!" Of course, he's mad. Why the hell wouldn't he be pissed. He just walked in and found me with my fingers buried deep, rubbing my nipples while inhaling his scent. This may be the only time throughout my life I wish the earth would open up and swallow me whole.

My hands fly up to cover my scarlet-colored face wishing I would have just suffered through the evening. Throbbing clit and all.

"I said no, and what I meant when I said this is don't stop."

"What?" I ask as I peek at him from under my hands.

He slips his shirt off and kicks off his boots. With his jeans hung low on his hips, I have the perfect view of the v disappearing down to the erection I can see pushing against his jeans, making me lick my lips from the anticipation. With his full attention focused on me, he confirms what he wants in a tone that leaves no doubt this demand comes from my Alpha, but the desire I hear comes only from my mate.

"I want you to finish what you started while I watch."

When my hands remain over my cheeks, he growls. "Shay, take the fucking covers off, return your fucking fingers to the pussy I plan to devour after you're done, and make yourself come while I watch."

As embarrassing as it was to have him catch me mid-act, knowing my effect over him erases this sentiment and sends me soaring back to the throbbing need that put me in this position. With my one arm still draped over my eyes, I slide my hand back down, circling my clit several times before I return them to where they were when he walked in.

"Take your arm away from your face and look at me while you slide your fingers inside that perfect pussy of yours," he demands. This isn't the first time I've masturbated, but it's the first time I've had an audience while I did it. But when he growls again, I know I've made him wait as long as he will allow. So I drop my arm as my gaze slowly lifts to meet his.

He's leaning against the door with his arms crossed, but his chest's rapid rise and fall tells me he isn't as in control as he wants me to believe he is. My hand working me at a steady pace, coupled with his hungry eyes watching, has me on the brink again in no time.

"When you come, Shay, don't hold back. I want to hear how much you miss me. How much you wish it was my fingers between those slick folds. Scream for me, beautiful."

My hand moves faster, exploring myself in ways I never have before, and when I drop the hand I was using to cover my eyes to my nipples to apply the pressure I need to send me crashing over the edge, I do exactly what he asked of me. I scream his name.

I'm still riding the waves of euphoria when he marches over and pulls my hand from between my legs before licking my fingers clean of the come coating them.

Episode One-Hundred Fourteen: Proclaim

Foster

I NEVER EXPECTED to discover Shay pleasuring herself in my bed, but the second I saw it, there was no fucking way I was going to let her stop. As much as I wanted it to be my hand, my tongue, or my cock doing it, watching her was almost as satisfying. Besides, witnessing how she moved her hand while she masturbated taught me the best way to please her the next time I do it.

With the image of her fingers fucking her sweet pussy playing on repeat, I lick every drop of come from them before I bury my cock deep inside her. With every thrust I give, she meets me with an upward lunge of her own as she bites the spot on my neck I am waiting for her to sink her fangs in.

Having sex with Shay is better than any other time I've been with someone, but if everything I'm hearing is true, then the sensation and sensitivity only increase after you mark your mate. Honestly, I'm not sure how much more I can take. Just the feel of her wrapped around my cock sends me into a frenzy. I have to work extremely hard not to ravage her whenever I'm with her.

Before I pass the point of no return, I pull out of her and drag her pussy to my mouth. She never has trouble getting wet for me, but today she isn't just wet... she is fucking soaked, and my tongue circling her clit only adds to the excitement I plan to lap up after she comes again.

"Jesus fucking Christ, Foster," she moans, which causes a groan from me. The vibration from this increases her pleasure, resulting in her pulling my face closer as she frantically grinds against it.

"Come for me, beautiful."

"Yes." Her legs tense, and her breath hitches, followed by her scream as the orgasm overtakes her, flooding her body with pleasure.

Not one to let the high she is riding fade away, I flip her over, yank her ass up and plunge my cock back into the pussy, still pulsing from her climax. My eyes shift to where I want my dick to remain for the rest of my days. Every time I slide out, I see the glistening sheen of her orgasm coating my cock.

"Have I ever told you how sexy it is watching my cock sliding in and out of you?"

"No," she pants as she pushes up on all fours.

"I wish you could see it. Maybe next time, I'll fuck you in front of a mirror so you can watch too."

"I want that," she confirms as she straightens so she can wrap her arms around the back of my neck, which brings those perfect tits of hers up for my viewing pleasure. With the fingers of one hand digging into her hip, I reach up with the other to play with her tits, rolling her rock-hard nipples against them. The moan she gives me as her hand drops to skim along my cock every time I pull out has me chasing the high she wants to grant.

"If you keep doing that, I'm going to fucking explode, Shay."

"I know I want you to come with me this time, and I'm so damn close."

Picking up my pace, I suck in shallow breaths as every muscle prepares for the rush of dopamine my brain is ready to release. My hand moves from her hip to press against her clit as she shudders around me. This is the last thing I need. With one final thrust, I reach the peak and spill my release.

After lying in the aftermath of our climax, Shay announces she needs to take a quick shower. I prop myself up, wanting to watch one of the most perfect asses to ever grace this planet walk into the bathroom.

I leave her alone for several minutes after I hear the shower turn on until thoughts of her running her hands over her wet body have me walking in behind her. I place a gentle kiss against her cheek before grazing my lips along her neck, but when I reach the spot I want more than anything else, I abruptly pull away.

"What are you doing? Why did you stop?"

"Because if I keep kissing you here, I won't be able to stop Shadow from marking you. The longer we are together, the harder it becomes to stop him from claiming you. From declaring to everyone that you are ours, which I won't do until you are ready to be ours forever. Both as my mate and my wife."

She slowly turns to face me, kissing me softly against my chest before whispering, "So don't."

"Don't mark you?" I ask, almost afraid of what she will say, but I need to know either way.

"Stop. Don't stop."

"Does this mean?"

"I'll marry you."

*****

Because I had no intention of completing the marking ceremony in my damn shower, I swept Shay into my arms to carry her back to my bedroom. Should I give her a second to reconsider? Is her agreement only because of the hormones still racing through her? I suppose the answer to this could be yes.

"Are you sure this is what you want, Shay? I need to know because there is no turning back once we do this."

"I know."

"And you're sure this is what you want?"

"I love you, Foster." I suck in a sharp breath, hearing her say this for the first time. "I always have, and I should have told you that when you told me how you felt, but I was scared. The only thing I'm afraid of now is living without you. So yes, I know what this means. And yes, I am prepared for what it entails. But most importantly, I'm ready and want to commit my heart and soul to you and only you."

I don't think I could be any happier than I am right now. I've been waiting to hear her say this since the day I stood in her house holding the note she wrote to tell us goodbye. With my hands against her cheeks, I lean forward to kiss the only woman I have ever loved.

"I need to tell you one thing before we do this."

Marcelle Valentine

"You can tell me anything, Shay. I learned my lesson the hard way, and I promise no matter what you say, I'll always listen, and it won't change anything."

"I don't know how to do this."

"The marking ceremony?"

"Yeah. No one ever told me how, and when I asked Ness, she told me to follow your lead, but this is too important not to know what I'm doing."

"It's okay, sweetheart. We'll first commit our souls to one another while asking the Moon Goddess to bless our union."

"What if she doesn't?"

"Bless our union?"

"Yeah."

"Then I tell her to fuck off and claim the only woman I love without her consent, but something tells me we don't have anything to worry about."

"So after we do that, what else?"

Running her finger over the spot on my neck, I tell her. "Then you'll let your fangs drop enough to be able to pierce my skin right where your finger is."

"I don't know if I know how to do that."

"I'll help you."

"Will it hurt?"

"I'm told it's rather pleasurable."

"But you don't know for sure?"

"Since you only do this once, I don't have first-hand knowledge, but I trust the people who told me."

"Okay, then what?"

"Then I'll do the same thing to you," I say as I run my finger over the spot Shadow has wanted me to bite since we first saw her.

"That's it?"

"After we have both marked the other, we'll complete the ritual while we consummate our binding and complete the mark on the other."

"So we bite each other while we make love."

"Basically, yes."

"Are we vampires?" She asks with a giggle.

"Not quite, but I imagine if a vampire has a marking ceremony, it would be similar."

"Okay, so we ask the moon goddess for permission while we make a vow to each other. Then I bite you, followed by you biting me. Then the fun stuff starts so we can complete the mark, which you have assured me will not hurt."

"That's about the long and short of it."

"Then I'm ready."

About damn time you do something right, blue balls.

Not even your stupid name can ruin this for me, furball. But I agree it is about time.

I take her hand and lead her out to the balcony. She lets out a small gasp when I sit down abruptly and pull her onto my lap. Her nerves get the better of her as she begins gnawing on her lower lip as her eyes move from me to the skies above us.

"Ready?"

"Yes."

"Just repeat what I say, okay?"

"Uh-huh." Her eyes once again search the skies.

Bringing her focus down to me, I begin the ceremony that will soon bind me to this beautiful soul. "I, Foster Brannon, choose Shay Andrews as my mate. I declare this before the Moon Goddess and ask you to grant our union."

"I, Shay Andrews, choose Foster Brannon as my mate. I declare this before the Moon Goddess and ask you to grant our union."

"We pledge our life, love, and entire existence to honor and protect our mate above all others."

"We pledge our life, love, and entire existence to honor and protect our mate above all others."

The words no sooner leave Shay's lips when the moon emerges from behind a cloud and silhouettes Shay in a silvery glow. Making my mate not only beautiful but breathtaking while confirming what I already knew... our union pleases the Goddess.

For the next part, I don't want anything between the woman I am pledging my life to and me. My fingers grasp the towel before pulling it away from her as I allow it to slide from my fingers.

"You have to concentrate on only letting a small piece of Moon out. When you feel your fangs descend, stop."

She does what I ask before she leans forward and pierces the spot that will bind us together for all eternity. I brush her long unruly hair aside before running my finger along her jaw. When I have her attention, I lean forward and finally grant Shadow his wish. I claim my mate.

Even though she gasps when I do this, I know it has nothing to do with pain because I can assure you what I felt had nothing to do with discomfort. Her lips are on mine the instant I pull away.

"I love you, Foster."

"I'll love you until time ends, beautiful."

I learn what true euphoria means when she lowers herself on my dick while I sink my fangs into her as she does the same to me.

Episode One-Hundred Fifteen: Moving

Shay

I DON'T KNOW what I was expecting to happen, but what we did was the furthest thing from everything I imagined, and I can't stop the smile, knowing I am his fated, chosen, and declared mate.

Not even Riona can ruin my high. Even as she tries again to convince him how wrong I am and how right she is as his mate.

"Let me make you dinner tonight. Then I'll show you what it's like to be with a woman who knows what you need rather than a wallflower who doesn't have the first clue how to please a man like you."

"No."

"Why not?"

"Because Shay and I have plans."

"Certainly nothing you can't put aside for one night."

"Riona, I've tried to be nice. I've tried to ignore you before moving onto anger, but nothing I do seems to get through to you, so now I'm going for direct—"

Before he can say whatever he wants to tell her, she smashes her lips to his. I almost shift to allow Moon a chance to rip her apart. She gloats when he pulls her arms from around his neck but keeps her hands held until he finishes what he wants to tell her.

"I accept your petition to join Ash Rock," her eyes slowly glide over to mine as she casts a cocky grin in my direction. Now I'm fucking confused. Why would he willingly bring a woman who almost ruined us into the pack?

"As your Alpha, I reject your request to be my mate. I refuse all advances you make. I demand you accept your position within my pack, but mostly I expect you to show your Luna the fucking respect she deserves. The next time you disparage Shay, my action will be swift and something I promise you will not like nor want."

Riona rips her hands from his, looking over at me and then back to him. As an official member of Ash Rock, she cannot refuse her Alpha unless she intends to be chased out of town.

"You mean to tell me she—"

"Finally granted us our deepest desire and allowed me to mark her before the Goddess right after she agreed to be my wife."

"You have to be fucking kidding me. You could have me, and instead, you chose some fucking wallflower like her?"

This is the last straw. Knowing what I am preparing to do may likely lead to losing my job, my house, and a man I consider a stand-in dad doesn't stop me because I refuse to stand by any longer and watch the shit this bitch does. Storming to the other side of the bar, I grab her hair and yank her away from my mate. I don't think she realizes who has her until I slam my fist into her face several times.

"Aye, what the hell is going on out here?"

"It seems your niece isn't overly happy about who I propose to, and it seems my future wife doesn't care for another she-wolf kissing me."

"Riona," he yells. "Not a titter of wit, you damn egit'. No wonder she busted your lip. Yer lucky it wasn't your ass. Now go home, Riona. We'll discuss this further when I get there."

"Uncle Seamus!"

"Go. Home. Now," he growls as he points to the door. When she turns to look at me, the gloating is long gone, replaced by what I can only call hate. Her lips are pulled tight, revealing her teeth underneath, she narrows her eyes while her brows draw together, but her stance captures her true feelings. If she thought she could get away with hitting me, she would. I know she only refrains from following her wolf's demand because she fears Foster. It certainly doesn't have anything to do with any fear of me. She actually believes I would willingly stand here and let her hit me. That I wouldn't defend myself. She's sadly mistaken. I did say I'm done being everyone and anyone's fucking doormat.

"As for you, Titchy—"

"Seamus, I'm sorry I hit your niece. I understand if you—"

"Houl yer whisht. I need a wee half'n' 'fore we jump into this." He takes several gulps from the glass he poured before continuing. "Aye, I admit you hittin' her isn't the easiest thing to swallow, but she was askin' for it. I don't know what to do about her. Does me head in actin' the maggot this way. But what I can see is me niece got what she deserved. 'Sides, I haven't had a decent night's rest since she arrived. I want to help me sister out, but if she doesn't find other livin' arrangements soon, I'm gonna hafta send her back to Ireland."

"We might be able to help with that," Foster says as he wraps his arms around my waist.

"We can?" I ask as I look from Seamus over to him.

"We can. Riona can move into Shay's old house. She won't be needing it any longer."

"I won't?"

"Did you think I would want my wife living anywhere other than with me?"

"I guess I never really thought about it."

"Truly, I could have me house back without a lippy woman-child there to ruin my peace?"

Foster looks over at me, waiting for my answer. As anxious as Seamus appears while waiting for the response, Foster seems almost as confident I will grant it. When I nod my head, Seamus cheers as Foster kisses me.

****

"So you finally decided you couldn't live without us?" Finn asks as he kisses my cheek.

"I guess so," I confirm. Even though I may sound ambivalent about the entire situation, the truth is I can't imagine my life anymore without these people in it.

"Is this everyone?" Foster asks as he walks in carrying a bunch of boxes.

"Sadie is working at the hospital today," Finch says as he flips a cup into the air.

"Today is Colt's birthday, so I told Maggie not to worry about coming. We could handle it," Brady says as he wraps his arms around a smiling Ness.

"Is she okay?" I ask. Now I am more concerned about my friend than packing my house up.

"She's... I don't know."

"Well, that settles it. Let's pack this place up fast. Then we can go home and pull her ass out of bed." And this is why I love Ness. There is no way she will let Maggie face this day by herself. We're halfway finished packing when Foster's phone rings.

"Hey, Madge," he says as he switches his phone to the speaker to continue fixing the bed we may have broken during one of our more aggressive sexual encounters.

"Hi, kid, I hate to call and bother you, but I need a favor."

"What's up?"

"A damn pipe burst in the stock room. I can't figure out how to fix it, and we just got a huge shipment."

"Isn't Atlas around?"

"No, he and a bunch of the other guys ran up to the Denver chapter. Blaze is the only member who didn't go, and I want to call him about as much as I want a hole in my head." I don't know who this Blaze guy is, but based on Foster's laugh and the snarl in which Madge said his name, I'm going to take a shot in the dark here and say he's an asshole.

"I'm helping Shay, but I could send some of my guys over."

"That would be great. I'll need maybe three or four guys to help me move stock until we can get everything fixed." Madge says, but there is no way I'm letting someone who might half-ass this go when I know Foster will ensure it's done right.

"Bullshit, Foster, I think I can handle packing up the rest of the house. You need to take care of this for her."

"It's okay, kiddo, he can send—"

"No, Madge, Foster is leaving right now. Ness and I will finish packing everything up, and then we'll head over to get Maggie. Just let me know when you're done, and we'll meet you back here to load the boxes."

"I guess my future wife settled that. I'll be there in a few minutes," Foster says as he stands and brushes his pant legs off.

"You heard her. She needs more than just you, so take Finn and Brady too."

After Brady and Foss kiss Ness and me, we stay on the porch waving until they pull away. When the truck is out of sight, I look at Ness to fill her in on my plan.

"Let's get this shit finished and grab a couple of bottles of wine before we head over to pull Maggie out of bed."

"Couldn't have said it better myself, sis," Ness says as she loops her arm in mine.

Episode One-Hundred Sixteen: The Devil's in the Details

Foster

When we pull into the lot, I can't help laughing at the sight of Madge waiting for us as she dries her hands. I've known this woman for a long time, and I can say I've never seen her like this. Madge's clothes are soaked, but attempting to save her jeans, she has them rolled up to her knees, her hair is disheveled, and she has more makeup running down her cheeks than around her eyes.

"Thank god you boys finally got here," she yells as we climb out of my truck. We follow her into the bar and down the stairs, where Atlas has converted the basement into storage, complete with a small elevator to make moving the stock upstairs to the bar easier.

The room has roughly six inches of standing water, and Madge did everything she could to move as much product out of the affected area as possible.

"Finn, get that water shut off and see what we can do to fix it. Brady, we need to move all the lower stock out of the room. Madge, make sure nothing is covering the drains."

We each work to ensure Atlas doesn't lose more stock than what's already ruined. Fifteen minutes later, the water is off, the supplies are moved, and the drains are unclogged, allowing the standing water to drain from the room as I talk with Atlas.

"Of course, something like this would happen the minute we all leave town. Thanks for coming over, Foss. I owe you big time."

"No, you don't. You'd do the same for me."

"Can we fix the pipe?" I ask Finn as he comes in, drying his hands on the towel Madge handed him before accepting the drink she poured.

"No can do, Foss."

"Why not?"

"Because the damn pipe is busted clean through."

"How the hell did that happen?" Atlas asks.

"Don't know, man. It looks like someone kicked the shit out of it. The pipe is bowed in several places and broken in the middle, not by the coupling or union where I would expect to find a break. Damn crazy too, since the pipe looks relatively new."

"It is. I had everything replaced when I bought the club."

"Did you say someone kicked it?" Madge asks as she pours each of us another round.

"That's what it looks like, but it could have been from the last time you received supplies. I suppose if someone shoved the boxes hard enough... Nah, never mind, it was definitely something more deliberate than a damn box haphazardly tossed about."

"Madge, has anyone been in the club?"

"No one other than Bobby when he dropped off our supplies, but I was with him the entire time. He didn't kick anything. Some guy showed up right after Bobby left but never came in."

"What do you mean, showed up?" I know Atlas and Denver are on the run, so I don't think anything of it when unease creeps into his question.

"Some guy who knocked on the door when I was getting ready to confirm we received everything for our shipment."

"What did he want?"

"Dunno. He asked if you were here, and when I told him no, he asked when you would be back. When I inquired what his visit was in reference to, he said it was personal and wouldn't elaborate beyond that."

"Did he say anything else?" I ask, confused why anyone would arrive at an MC's door without making arrangements first. The whole situation is starting to feel off.

"Nope, just made some small talk about the town and how much work Atlas has done to the place. Then he thanked me and left."

"What did he look like? Was he dressed in black, specifically leather with a sigil on the sleeve?" Atlas is no longer trying to hide his concern.

"No, just jeans, a white t-shirt with a black fleece zip-up jacket." I hear Atlas release the breath he was holding. "He was taller, around six-foot, stocky build, short brown hair. As pleasant as he was with me, his eyes didn't match the sentiment. Kinda gave me the creeps, if you know what I mean."

"Did he leave a name?" I figure if he did, maybe it would clear this situation up.

"When he first started talking, he mumbled something like Trent, Trevor, Trey, something like that."

"Travis?" Brady asks her as he leaps from the barstool. And suddenly, my heart is in my throat.

"Yeah, that was it. Travis."

"Fuck, Finch, call the girls," I yell as Brady and I sprint out of the club.

*****

Skidding to a stop in front of the last place I left her, Brady and I race toward the house.

"Shay," I yell as I barge through room after room.

"Ness," Brady does the same from the outside.

When I call her phone, it rings multiple times before going to voice mail. I immediately switch gears and call Maggie's. I know Ness and Shay were both concerned about her well-being. With any luck, they left shortly after we did to check on her.

Maggie answers on the second ring, "Sorry, Foster, I know I said I would be there today, but—"

"Is Shay and Ness with you?" I ask, cutting her off.

"No. Why?"

"I'll call you back," I don't wait for her response as I hang up to try Ness's phone this time, but her's doesn't even ring.

"Anything, Foster?"

"No," I tell him as my apprehension slowly becomes fear. I frantically call Shay's number again, praying to the Moon

Goddess that she answers this time, and for a brief second, it seems my prayers have been granted when I hear the click of her phone being answered.

But the relief doesn't last long.

"Has anyone ever told you you should always keep your favorite playthings close at hand?"

"Maximus!"

"Now, something about how you said my name leads me to believe you aren't happy to hear from me."

"Where's Shay?"

"Close by."

"Where. Is. She?"

"Spending some quality time with my little brother. I gotta tell you, Foster, he isn't overly fond that you marked the bitch he has been chasing for years."

"If he fucking touches her—"

"You'll kill him? Yeah, I already told him as much. Your problem is he doesn't give a shit."

"I am coming for her. But not just Shay, I'm coming for you too."

"Oh, I'm counting on it. Talk to you soon, asshole." Before the phone goes quiet, I hear Ness's muffled cries, followed by Shay's faint screams.

Episode One-Hundred Seventeen: Kitten

Shay

*A*FTER WE TOSSED the last of my stuff into the boxes, Ness told me she'd be waiting for me in her car. I just wanted to do one more quick check of the house before locking everything up.

I can't believe I'm leaving the first home I ever called mine behind. I can certainly tell you this isn't what I imagined when I fled my pack all those months ago. I admit I can't stand the woman who will soon move in, but I love Seamus, and if this is how he will finally have some peace, then I'm happy to be doing this for him.

My phone alerts me to a new text. Figuring it's Ness telling me to get my ass moving, I lock the back door and grab my jacket. With one last look around the place, I open the door to my new life. The problem is fate seems to have other plans for me.

"Hello, kitten." I try to slam the door closed, but Max is on me faster than I can react. My only saving grace is he doesn't smash a rag filled with chloroform and wolfsbane against my face this time.

"Now, I know this is going to be hard since you're so feisty, but if you don't want your new friend hurt, I suggest you calm the fuck down."

Struggling out of his grip, I spin to face him as I growl, "Why are you doing this?"

"Because, kitten, like you, I have a soft spot for the people I care for, and as big of a pain in the ass as Travis can be, he's still my little brother."

"Where's Ness?"

"Trav is holding her as collateral to make sure you stay nice and compliant," Max says as he scratches his jaw.

"Let her go."

"No," he tells me in his calm, piss-you-off-without-trying manner.

"Why not?"

"Because I already told you she's collateral."

"For what?"

His heavy sigh, while he rubs his head, informs me my questions annoy him. Good. No one said I had to make this easy on him.

"Two-fold. It keeps your boyfriend in line and guarantees your compliance, including getting your ass moving. So chop-chop, kitten, we need to put some distance between your mate and us before nightfall."

With no other options, if I don't want to see Nessie hurt, I follow Max out to the truck parked on the road. No matter how much I want to pretend, I'm not afraid. The second Travis steps out of the waiting vehicle, my heart feels like it will pound through my ribcage. The last time I was with this fucker, he stabbed me so I wouldn't fight him when he tried to rape me. And I know if I climb into this truck, I will not walk away from this with only a scar from a knife wound.

If it wasn't for Max opening the back door to reveal a bound and crying Ness, I don't think I could have forced my feet to move any further.

"What's happening here?" I spin to find Seamus coming around the side of the house.

Max pushes the door closed to block Seamus's view of Ness as he warns me, "Don't do anything foolish, kitten."

"I ask ya a question."

"We're just—"

"None of your fucking business, old man. If you know what's good for you, you'll turn your ass around and head back in the same direction you came from."

The low growl Max gives Travis confirms he doesn't agree with his brother's stupid response. There's one thing I know about Seamus once you land on his bad side, there is no coming back.

"Or what, you bloody chancer?"

"Or—" Max hits Travis in the chest harder than necessary if you only want to get someone's attention. He did this to silence him.

"Just returned to town and stopped to see an old friend."

"That so, huh?"

"It is," Max says as a friendly smile slides across his face. I'm not sure who I'm more afraid of. Travis, with his hostile approach to life, or Max, who charms you before he shoves a

203

knife in your back. Crocodile or snake, you decide which is more deadly.

"It doesn't look like Titchy is all that happy about your impromptu visit. So I think she'll be comin' with me."

"I don't know about that. What do you say, Shay? Wanna come with us or go with him?"

"What are you playin' at, Maximus? You always were a bloody egit'. Suppose it's too much to hope you've changed."

"Now, Seamus, here I am being nothing but nice, and you have to go and insult me."

"Don't hurt him," I plead.

"Then get in the fucking truck," he snarls as he moves to put himself between Seamus and me. Hoping he'll understand how much trouble we're in, I open the door wide enough to reveal Ness inside. I figured he would wait until we pull away and call Foster, ya know, possibly send in the calvary, not try to take on two pissed-off shifters by himself. The problem is the second he sees her, he charges the two men, who have no problem attacking him.

Travis, by far, is the worst of the two, holding nothing back as he attacks the man trying to save us, but when Seamus gains the upper hand, Max is there to stop it. With one violent hit, Seamus collapses to the ground. While Travis drags him behind the house, Max calmly walks over to where I'm standing with my hand over my mouth.

"I saw what you did, kitten. I didn't appreciate it. Now get in the fuckin' truck." As Max holds the back door open for me, I look from side to side, hoping to find any means of escape, until I hear Ness cry.

"Shay?" Even if I shift and somehow manage to escape these assholes, it will leave Ness alone with them. I know Travis well enough to understand if I did this, Ness, not me, would be the one to suffer at his hands. For this reason alone, I climb into the truck.

As the door closes behind me, I see the happy life I've hoped for slipping away.

*****

Foster

How did I not see this shit coming? If anything happens to Ness or Shay, I'll never forgive myself for failing them.

"Did you finally realize you picked the wrong girl?" I spin around to find Riona standing beside my truck, twirling a strand of her hair.

"What the fuck are you doing here?"

"Looking for my uncle. He told me he was coming over here to check on the progress of the wallflower—pardon me, your chosen mate, but I never heard from him. So I decided to check on it myself."

"How long ago did he come over here?"

"Give or take about an hour and a half ago. But hey, since we're both here and it seems the house is empty, why don't you give me a tour?"

"Brady, look for any signs of a struggle," I say, ignoring the woman beside me.

"Foster, what's the word?" Finch pants as he rounds the corner.

"They're gone, but I think Seamus may have stumbled across them."

"What are you talking about? What did my uncle stumble across?" When I refuse to answer her, she presses further. "Let me guess, it has something to do with the bitch you claimed."

"If you fucking—" I snarl, but before I can finish, Finch puts his hand on my shoulder and shakes his head.

"Not worth it, brother. Let's focus on what does matter."

"Finch, Foster, over here," Brady yells from behind the house. As much as I don't want Riona involved with this shit, she follows us as we bolt to where he is squatted. I can't believe the shape we find Seamus in. It looks like someone took a baseball bat to his head. Lifting him up, we gingerly carry him inside to tend to his wounds away from the watchful eyes of his neighbors.

Once inside, he slowly regains consciousness, and what he tells us sets my teeth on edge.

"Max and his brother took her. She stood not four meters before me, and I couldn't reach her in time."

"Did they hurt her? Force her to leave with them?"

"No, she climbed into the truck of her own accord."

"What? You're telling me she went willingly?"

"Don't know how willing she was."

"I'm not following."

"Titchy isn't the only one they took. They have Nessie too."

Episode One-Hundred Eighteen: Fleeing

Max

TRAVIS'S ANXIOUS ENERGY is driving me fucking crazy. I know it has everything to do with the girl he wants to fuck in the back seat. But if he continues to drum his hands on his thighs, I'm going to rip those fucking hands from his wrists.

"How much longer before we stop for the night?"

"You need to exercise a modicum of patience, little brother."

"I think I've waited long enough," he growls as he looks over his shoulder at the woman clinging desperately to the only reason she agreed to come with us.

"I say we stop now." He shifts so he can push his growing erection down.

"Four hours is all that separates us from certain fuckin death, so I don't care how desperate you are to get your dick wet. We aren't stopping until that gap has grown exponentially."

"Listen, after I break her in a couple times, we can tag team her. Maybe she's like Erin, and she'll moan like a whore as I fuck her sweet ass while she chokes on your dick."

"Moaning like a whore isn't my thing. At least not where you're concerned," Shay mumbles as she looks out the window. Her comment makes me laugh; unfortunately, Trav doesn't find it as amusing as I did.

"That's because you've never been fucked by me yet. But trust me, when my brother and I take you... you will moan like the whore you are, Shay."

"I've already told you once, little brother, I don't stick my dick anywhere biting teeth can remove it."

"And I told you it's a simple fix. We knock her damn teeth out of her mouth. Problem fuckin' solved."

At least with his attention focused on Shay and adjusting his pants to make room for his growing dick, I have a minute's peace to contemplate our next move. I never intended on Foster knowing we were the ones who took her. But when Seamus showed up, I knew my planned anonymity was a distant wish I would never achieve. For this reason, I turn right instead of left when we arrive at the proverbial fork in the road.

"Wait, why did you turn this way? Aren't we going back to the pack house?"

"Where do you think the first fucking place Foster will look for us?"

"The packhouse."

"Well, give that man a prize," I say in my best carnival barker's voice.

"Who fucking cares if some limp-dick Alpha shows up? We'll take care of him like we did his fuckin' brother."

"Might I remind you his brother is still alive, well, and probably tracking us with the limp-dick Alpha you don't know shit about?"

"Let's get one thing straight, assholes. Foste's dick is thick, huge, hard, and fills me perfectly," Shay snarls while his cousin winces, having to hear about his cock.

Travis lurches to hit her, but I halt his attack when I yank him back on his seat. This idiot needs to learn the way of the world he is dipping his toe in. "You need to learn one thing: Foster is not a wolf to be taken lightly."

"Aren't you the smart one?" Shay mumbles again. I have to say her snarky attitude is growing on me. My eyes find hers looking directly at me through my rearview mirror. I never realized before how blue her eyes are. I like it.

"Fuck it. I still say we go home. What the hell was the purpose of taking the pack if we're just going to abandon it now?"

"No one said I'm deserting anything. But do you really want to be there with your dick in hand when he shows up to reclaim his mate, or how about Brady? Because after the conversation I overheard while you were getting your beauty sleep, it seems we have his mate too."

"No shit, you're Brady's mate? Damn, maybe I'll take you too. Teach that little fucker a lesson."

"I can't wait to watch Foster kill you," Ness snaps as Shay pulls her closer.

"I'm not afraid of either of those pricks."

"And that is why you'll die young. You're too fuckin' dumb to admit your deficiencies. Foster and Brady each represent one," I tell him as clearly as possible. He needs to learn his boundaries. I've tried to make him understand this for years, but this dumb little shit refuses to listen to reason. I'm tired of cleaning up his messes, and I'm sick of pulling his ass out of the fire.

Perhaps I won't intercede on his behalf when Foster catches up with us because one thing I am absolutely sure of... a confrontation is looming on the horizon.

*****

Atlas

One desperate call from Foster is all it took to get me moving toward the place he found Shay last time. My mission is to watch and let him know when they return. If they return. While he, Brady, and Finch drive here from Colorado.

It doesn't matter that the Vanguard has been circling Denver and me. Foster's mate and my new friend Shay wouldn't be in this situation had I not left so suddenly, sending Foster rushing over to my clubhouse to help Madge when she needed it.

It seems everything circles back to the club, Denver, and me. I will continue watching the packhouse, but I won't hesitate to rescue Shay and Ness if I see an opportunity to do it without them getting hurt. I'm not worried about the wolves in this pack; they don't stand a chance against someone like me. I am the first of my father's sons, a warrior, and the one in charge of his honor guard. I didn't get this position because of my heritage; I won it through sweat, blood, and hard work. I did it to prove myself to my father, assure him I would never let him down, and would always protect our kind.

If Ayaan hadn't poisoned my father, I would be there now battling any who thought our kingdom was easy pickings, and like all the other races before them, I would stand victorious as I showed them the error of their misguided attempt. My kind has toppled forces far greater than what my father's kingdom possesses, and none have ever defeated us.

So facing a few wolves is the least of my concerns. This does not come from a place of arrogance. This comes from centuries of battle experience to protect what we hold dear.

As much as I want to be out hunting Ayaan right now, this is where I need to be. But Ayaan's day is coming.

Episode One-Hundred Nineteen: Brothers

Shay

*A*S SCARED AS I am, I have to portray strength for Ness. She's never been in a situation like this before, and the last thing I need her to do is freak out until I figure out how to get us both out of this shitty situation.

Escape wasn't an option because we were never far from one of the brothers, and the few times we were, they separated us, knowing neither Ness nor I would run without the other.

Max and Travis seem at odds with one another about how to best handle things. Travis wants nothing more than for Max to pull over so he can carry out his base desire to make me suffer and scream. While Max is more methodical. Not to mention the only person currently standing between Travis and me. It's only because of him I haven't had to fight Travis off me yet. Max has yanked him back up front each time he has tried to climb back here.

As far as I'm concerned, this doesn't make him a good guy, just not as monstrous as Travis. But it makes me wonder how long it will be before Travis uses Ness against me to get what he wants. I know he will. Eventually, he will wise up and realize Ness is the only way I will comply.

It's been three days since they took us, and we've been on the road for most of it. This is the only reason Travis hasn't had the chance to carry out his plans. But tonight, Max has decided to get rooms so he can get some sleep. I guess sleeping in the front seat of his truck isn't as comfortable as curling up in the back seat. And since every time Travis attempts to climb back here, Maximus is there to stop him, it doesn't lend much in the way of rest. But what am I supposed to do tonight when Max is asleep in his room, and I'm chained up in mine?

Since opening the door and climbing into his truck for the first time, I fear what will happen when no one else is around us. To keep Travis happy, Max allowed him to choose the hotel, which happens to be a fleabag, pay-by-the-hour we-overlook screaming women kind of place. While I'm not used to staying at some fancy five-star hotel, this place is shadier than I want to sleep at.

I suppose it shouldn't surprise me the room Travis shoves me into is directly next to his while Ness is hauled to the other end where Max will be staying.

"I'm not screwing around with you, little brother. Go to bed." When Travis tries to enter my room, Max grabs his arm before growling, "In your fucking room."

If Travis could string a coherent sentence together through his angry tirade, I think it would have gone something like this: *I've been waiting for years. You fuckin' promised me I could have her. This is the entire reason we collected her so that I could finally fuck this bitch.* Or something close to this.

"Don't make me say it again, Travis."

But Max is unrelenting as he stands there waiting to ensure Travis doesn't bolt into my room the second his back is turned. If he is so damn worried about it, why did he put me next to this asshole? The last thing I see before Travis storms into his room is Max standing at the other end, watching us with Ness struggling to break out of his grip.

Slipping through the door, I hear something thud against the wall before his voice filters through the vent. "Be seeing you soon, Shay."

I check the locks again before shoving a chair under the door handle. With the lights out, I press my back into the corner of the room to keep my eyes on both the door and the window. But the warning Max gave Travis was enough to keep him from bothering me. The problem is that Max bangs on my door shortly after sunrise, telling me it's time to rise and shine. Rise and shine, shit, I haven't even closed my eyes yet.

 The next day he pulls up in front of a house he announces as home sweet home. I can promise you this there is nothing sweet about this shit hole. And like the night at the hotel, they refuse to let Ness stay in the same room as me.

The bedroom they stuck me in has all the windows boarded over and locks on both sides of the door. Although the ones on my side are flimsy compared to the flip side.

I am only vaguely aware the hour is late, but this is because when Max collected me for dinner, it was almost nine o'clock, and that was hours ago. So when I hear the clicking of locks, I fear who it may be. I scamper out of bed, not wanting this asshole to find me in it if Travis happens to be the one coming through my door. All my nightmares are realized when he enters the room and locks the door behind him.

"Alone at last." The gloating grin he gives me infuriates me more than his appearance.

"Max isn't going to like you defying him."

"My brother," he mocks. "Isn't going to find out. At least not until after the deed is done. Now you can make this easy on yourself, or we can do it the fun way."

"Of course, you would think forcing yourself on someone is fun." As hard as I try to control my expression, I can't help it when my lip twists up and my nostrils flare with disgust.

"I did say it was your choice."

"Stay the fuck away from me," I spat as I circle the edge of the room.

"Tsk-tsk," he says with a click of his tongue. "Oh, and just so you know, I plan to claim the useless bitch down the hall. After I'm done with you. You get to be the first."

"Leave Ness alone," I screech.

"No. I don't think I will."

"I'm warning you!"

"What are you going to do about it, Shay? I'll tell you what... not a fucking thing because after I've had my fill of fucking you in every way you have ever fantasized about," I whip my head up. The utter disgust covering my face has to be clear. "I don't plan on letting you walk back out of here. So really, Shay, how do you plan on stopping me?"

Travis stalks towards me. When he is within striking distance, he grabs my throat, squeezing to the point any hope of taking another breath is wrenched out of my lungs as his mouth smashes against mine. He punches me when I try to pull away before viciously biting my lip. Refusing to react to his abuse, he slams his head against my cheek. Blinding white lights flash across my field of vision, and this time I cannot help but cry out as pain rips through my face.

His hand squeezes my breast in his excruciating vice-like grip. He is not gentle, and like the pain I felt from his last hit, agony consumes my every thought as I fight not to scream from the abuse he doles out. My wolf desperately tries to claw her way out, frantic to help me. He rips my pants off before I can stop him and throws me back onto the bed. The worst part is the sound of his zipper as tooth after tooth it pulls apart.

"Yeah, I didn't think you would do anything to stop me," he says, licking my face.

"Who said Shay's the one who will fucking stop you?" My eyes shoot over Travis's shoulder, only to discover Max standing in the doorway.

Travis pushes off the bed but does not leave.

"I told you not to put your hands on her. And what do you do the first opportunity you get? You try to fuck her." Max storms further into the room, slamming his hands into Travis's chest, sending Travis toppling over the bed while I scramble to escape their fight.

I don't get far before Max has me tossed over his shoulder as he moves toward the room's exit. This is until Travis charges Max, who has to sidestep his furious brother's incoming assault while I can only hope to avoid taking the hit he intended for Max. He plops me down into the corner before saying, "Stay put, kitten."

For all of Travis's bluster, Max easily subdues him. It's almost shocking to witness as Travis charges, and Maximus flips around in some crazy superhero move to lock his neck tightly inside the crook of his arm. After Travis slumps to the floor groaning, Max carries me into his room before tossing me on his bed.

I scurry back against the headboard, afraid I traded one brother for another. This thought seems to confirm itself when Max begins undressing. I admit when he climbs into bed next to me before turning away from me, I can't help but feel relief flood through me.

"Lie down, Shay," he demands, shoving the pillow further under his head. When I refuse to do as he asks, he sits up on his knees and yanks me down until I have no other choice than to flop back against the bed. Before I can right myself, he moves over the top of me.

"If you don't want to be my brother's play toy tonight, I suggest you stay put."

"Where's Ness?"

"Safe. Someplace Travis can't get to her for now."

"For now?"

"Yes, Kitten, for now. How long she stays that way depends on you and your willingness to behave." He leans closer, pressing his lips against my ear before continuing. "Like right now, when I'm trying to get some rest." After he says this, he pulls his pillow to lie directly beside me. If I move an inch, hell a toe, I'll be against him.

"What are you doing?"

"In case you get any bright ideas. Thoughts like trying to find Ness."

"I promise I won't try anything if you tell me where she is."

"And what would you be trying, kitty-cat?"

"Not whatever the hell you're thinking," I figure my comment will piss him off, but rather than rage, I receive a laugh. Deciding to see how long I can push this, I ask him another question.

"Can I ask you something?"

"Certainly."

"Why were you not a member of Half Crest?"

"Are you thinking about the time you missed out on being with me? All those years we could have been—"

"No! I'm wondering why Travis was there, but you weren't."

He pushes up so he can look down at me. "Simple. I remained with my mom."

"I thought your mom died when you and Travis were little? At least that's what Travis always said."

"I was young but not little, kitten. When my dad left, Travis was too little to remember shit, and I'm sure any of Travis's memories had something to do with my dad's version."

"Meaning?"

"Dad probably told him this shit to keep him from looking for her or me."

"But he found you."

"More like I stumbled across him when we were teens. While I knew who he was right away, he only figured it out when I mistakenly linked my mind to his. We kept in touch after dad passed away."

"Do you mind me asking what happened?"

He lifts a strand of my hair and twirls it between his fingers. "My parents decided it would be best if they separated."

"Why?"

"So they didn't kill one another."

"Was it really that bad?"

He smiles as he drops my hair to run his fingers along my jaw. "Let's just say my mom wasn't the easiest person to love.

218

Trav went with him when my dad left, while I stayed with my mom."

"You didn't get along with your dad?"

"Quite the opposite. I loved and admired him."

"So why stay with your mom?"

"Because she was my mom, and someone needed to do it. Someone had to protect her from the other wolves as much as from herself. So dad returned to his pack while mom and I became rogue."

"Why didn't you find your dad after she died?"

"Too much time. Too much space. I wasn't the same kid I was when he left me behind, so I figured it was best for everyone involved if I stayed away."

"But you were just a kid. And rogue."

"There are worse things than being rogue." He says as he runs his finger over my lips. "Did I satisfy your inquiring mind, kitten?"

"Yes."

"So, can I finally get some rest?" My nod lets him lie back down, but to my amazement, when he drops onto the bed beside me, he pulls me against him. Keeping his arm resting across my abdomen.

"Max...."

"Yes, kitten."

"I'm sorry about your mom... your dad... everything."

"You didn't do anything to owe me an apology... well, besides not allowing me to get some sleep."

"I only have one more question."

"Of course you do." He says, and surprisingly, I don't hear anger in his tone. It's amusement.

Marcelle Valentine

"How can you be so sure Travis can't get to Ness." He props himself up on one arm to look down at me as he sweeps the hair from my face.

"Because for him to get to Ness, he has to come through here, and I promise he isn't so keen to challenge me again tonight. So how about you give me a break and let me get some sleep, kitten?"

When I don't argue any further, he lies back down and pulls me against him before whispering, "No wonder they all want you so damn bad. You smell delicious."

My eyes snap open only to find him gazing at me. A low chuckle reverberates from his chest to my side, and once again, I question if I just traded one brother for another.

Episode One-Hundred Twenty: Indifferent

Foster

UNLIKE THE LAST time I came here looking for her, I don't need anyone to show me where the fuck she is this time. So it should come as no surprise when I refuse to slow my truck down and opt to barrel through the gate instead.

Atlas did as I asked and stayed out of sight while watching for her arrival. I know I told him he didn't have to do anything else, but he assured me if he saw them, nothing would stop him from retrieving Ness and Shay.

My truck has no sooner skidded to a stop when Brady, Finch, and I are out and stalking toward their Alpha house. Throughout our trip to reach this place, Brady fills us in on everything he knows about Travis while Finn and I provide details about Max.

This is why I forgo the pack house in favor of the Alpha house. These two brothers like to believe themselves special. They are about to find out how incredibly wrong they are.

"Who the fuck are you?" one sentinel growls as we approach. I don't have fucking time to deal with the likes of him, so when the punch I deliver knocks him on his ass, I believe he receives my message loud and clear.

Without stopping, I provide him with sound advice. "Stay down if you don't want me to do it again."

"What the fuck are you doing here, Brady?" Now this asshole, I remember. He's the same fucker who tried to pull Shay away from me the last time I came here to get her. What was his fucking name?

"Where the fuck are our mates, Pete?" Yeah, that's his name. The last time I was here, Petey boy ended up on his ass; this time, I don't plan on being as nice.

I pounce when he opens his mouth, and the first snarky word tumbles out. The sound of his nose breaking as I repeatedly hit him was like music to my ears. I don't stop there; I continue hitting him until he crumples on the ground before me.

Finch stops him by grabbing his shirt when he tries to scramble away from us. "Where did you fucks take my sister and my Luna?"

"Who the hell are you talking about?" He asks as he throws his arm up to protect his head if Finn decides to deal with him as I did.

"My sister, Vanessa or Ness, and my Luna, Shay," Finn repeats himself slowly, taking his time to enunciate each word, wanting to ensure this is the last time he has to say it.

"That fucking bitch is a Luna?" Finn returns to full height. His focus settles on me while a laugh tumbles out of him. This shouldn't have put the asshole at ease. But it did.

"Bitch," Finn repeats as he points down at the man looking from him to me. Before he can lift his arm again, Finch raises his foot and slams it directly into his face.

When Brady moves towards him, he must have thought he wanted to hit him too, but unlike Finn and me, Brady yanks him to his feet before straightening his shirt, "Pete, it would be in your best fucking interest to tell me where those two assholes took the girls. Because if you don't, I promise this... you will find out why my father was going to name me the Alpha of this fucked up pack."

"They left almost two weeks ago and haven't returned."

"This is the best intel you can provide," I growl as I move to hit him again.

"I said they haven't returned, but I can find out where they're hiding."

"Good man. Now we're getting somewhere. Shall we?" I say as I point him toward the Alpha house.

*****

Shay

I'm still trying to wrap my head around what happened last night. After Max pulled me against him, he went to sleep. He may have been comfortable... I wasn't. Not because I thought he would pick up where Travis left off. Something told me this wasn't what he intended. Despite that, men like Max don't do anything out of the kindness of their hearts. Now I suppose it's up to me to piece this together without pissing him off... and preferably before he changes his mind and lets his brother carry out his darkest desires.

"I don't understand. Why did you do that last night?"

"Do what?"

"Keep your brother from...."

"Raping you?" A shiver runs up my spine hearing someone else say this. "Because regardless of what you think of me, I'm not as big of an asshole as you might believe."

"You aren't," the laugh I give is more *yeah right* than humor.

"No, kitten, I'm not," he says, stepping closer into my space. "Besides, I couldn't stand the thought."

"Thought of him raping someone?"

"Thought of him touching you."

"What?"

"Do you really want me to elaborate on that?" His thumb grazes over my cheek as his eyes drop to my lips. He has stunned me into silence, and I don't know how to answer his question.

"Because I will if you want the truth. Just make sure you're ready for what I tell you." The cocky grin I'm used to finding on his face returns when I shake my head. It doesn't take a genius to figure out what he's insinuating. This man abducted me so his brother could have his way with me, only to turn around and stop him at every opportunity. Talk about a damn enigma.

"Why did you attack Brady's pack?"

"It was your pack too."

"Not anymore."

"I'm every bit the asshole your boyfriend believes I am."

"But you keep doing things to contradict this."

"Don't let my good guy act fool you. Because I'm not a nice man, Shay."

"Colton was."

"Colton was what?"

"A nice guy."

"They normally are, kitten."

"Why do you keep calling me that?"

"Honestly?" when I nod, he tells me something I was unprepared for. "I like watching the heat in your eyes every time I do it."

With me stunned silent, Max jerks his head at the door but waits for me to exit before he follows me out. His casual, indifferent posture and pace are somewhat off-putting. I'm used to him being a sarcastic asshole... an aloof sarcastic asshole, but an asshole all the same. Not this attentive and compassionate man. When we enter the kitchen, I find Ness already there waiting for us, and the spread he set up across the table is enough to satisfy anyone. Thankfully, Travis is nowhere to be seen.

After a week of being with this man, I'm less terrified of what Travis wants to do and more afraid of what Max is trying to do.

Episode One-Hundred Twenty-One: Choices

Max

*T*RAVIS LEFT SHORTLY after I took Shay away from him. I know he's pissed, and I suppose he has every right to be. The issue is I don't give a fuck. This girl somehow got under my skin, and the thought of him using her as his play toy infuriated me. I recall once saying there are some women I deem only worthy of sucking my dick, while others I want on it.

Shay represents the latter.

I had planned on returning to the pack I claimed, but now I'm unsure I want to let her go. At least not yet, and I know if I return, it will be to face Foster. Which is something else I'm not ready to do. It seems this prick has the soul of a cat or, at the very least, the nine lives of one. This bastard has been a thorn in my side since I arrived in Lake.

Foster is an issue for another time. Right now, I need to figure out where the hell Travis went. Thanks to my mom asking me on her deathbed to look after him, he is my problem. Travis has always been a shit, but he's my little brother, and as convinced as he is that he can handle any situation, I'm not as confident.

After assuring the women ate, and they were securely back in their rooms, I slipped out to find Trav. My first call is to my trusted scout Henry.

Per my directive, he does not say my name when he answers the phone, instead giving me a cursory. "Henry."

"Any news?"

"We have a spy."

"I figured it wouldn't take long. Any ideas who our visitor is?"

"Prick from Lake. I would have never seen the big fucker if not for the rain. I picked up his silhouette."

"Is Rich still in Colorado?"

"Sure is, and already on it, boss." I knew I liked him. The already-on-it reference is regarding the coke that will find its way into Atlas's clubhouse just before the local police receive a tip informing them the first shipment for the club's cushy new drug-running business has arrived. Can't have Atlas reporting all my comings and goings to Foster.

"Has Trav shown up there?"

"He isn't with you?"

"I pissed him off last night when I took his plaything, and he took off."

"Haven't seen him yet, but if he shows up. You'll be the first to know."

After hanging up, I grab some supplies before returning to the house we are staying in. A shit hole I bought a long time ago for situations like this. After I put everything away, I stroll upstairs only to discover the door to Shay's room is open, and the space is in shambles. As if a struggle occurred in there. I know Travis and I had a tussle in here last night, but the room was not in this state when I left her here this morning.

Jogging to the room I have Ness held in, I find her sobbing on the floor when I rush in.

"Where the fuck is she?"

"He took her."

"Who?" I don't need her to answer this; I already know. There is only one *he* who would take only Shay out of here if they were discovered, but I still need to hear her say it.

"Your damn brother, who the hell do you think? He came in and took her out of here screaming."

"When?"

"Thirty minutes ago."

"Stay put," I growl as I storm out of the room while she informs me...

"He wasn't alone."

*****

Shay

When I heard someone coming up the stairs, I thought Max had returned with Travis, but what I was faced with was much worse.

"After all this time, I finally will have my revenge," Adela declares as she dangles the collar she intends to put on me from her hand. Moon doesn't whimper. She releases an agonizing howl as she realizes what will happen soon. Pressing myself as far into the corner as possible, I scream for Foster and Brady. I

228

beg Travis not to let her do this. I call out when none of this works, hoping Max has returned. Hell, anyone would be welcome as long as they stop her from putting that thing on me.

It speaks volumes he went to the one person he knew would help him claim me and how willing she was to work with one of the men who dethroned her son. It seems these two care about one thing more than vendettas or humiliations and just about anything else... which is torturing me.

I try to dodge Travis's lunge, but he overpowers me with ease. I am vaguely aware of Ness screaming for them to leave me alone somewhere down the hall when the first scream rips from me. As hard as I struggle to keep the collar away from my neck, Travis is too strong, and with the help of Adela, it doesn't take long before Moon's screaming cries fill every corner of my mind.

I have brief periods when I come to after this, including when Travis rips my shirt and jeans off to allow Adela unobstructed access to whip me. The sting from the lash as it tears at my skin is nothing compared to what Moon is suffering, and my screams for her to fight often go unheard.

Everything becomes hazy from here. The beatings, Travis's hands on my body, his mouth against mine, Moon's screams. It's not until I hear Travis tell Adela to get out that I know he has reached the end of his patience, and if I have any hope of stopping him, I need to focus.

"Why you want this trash is something I will never understand."

"Because I want to take what your son always wanted but never had the balls to capture."

"My son never wanted this vile creature."

Marcelle Valentine

"Apparently, you don't know him half as well as I do because he panted for this bitch his entire life. It's only because of how much he wanted her that pushed me to take her for myself."

"I don't fucking believe you."

"You can leave or watch as I do what Brady always wanted. I don't care which, but I plan to fuck her until she screams my name." I try to yank away from the hand running up the inside of my thigh, only to discover I can't move. I'm tied to the damn table, and there is no room for escape this time.

As Travis begins to clamber over me, the door shatters, and my heart soars, believing Foster has found me, but I'm shocked when I look over and find Max filling the doorframe. The fury covering his face confirms he is not happy with Travis or Adela.

"Take the fucking collar off her," he growls at Adela.

"No!"

"No?"

"That's what I said. I have this bitch right where I want her. If you think I'm going to let you—" Max doesn't allow her to finish before he snatches out and breaks her neck, tossing her aside like nothing more than garbage. With this one act, he kills the woman who tormented me my entire life.

"Now I'll give you the same option I gave her. Take. The. Fuckin'. Collar. Off."

"You'd really kill your own brother over this bitch."

"Continue pressing your luck, and you'll find out." I hear Travis mumble something, but he does as Max instructs and cuts the collar away. I don't think this is how the thing is supposed to be removed because it feels like he has removed half my skin when the damnable thing falls away.

230

Before Travis can say anything else, Max punches him several times before Travis collapses, begging Max to stop the assault.

Max grabs Travis by the shirt, yanking Trav's face within inches of his before snarling, "I don't fucking share someone like her, little brother. The next time you put your damn hands on her, I'll cut the fucking things off."

After this, he rips the restraints away and covers me with his jacket before carrying me out of the room I thought I would meet my end in.

Episode One-Hundred Twenty-Two: The Confrontation

Foster

I DON'T HAVE to wait for this Pete to find them. The call I get from Atlas puts me on their trail. When I catch up to Max's truck, Atlas makes his move and drops in front of it, effectively boxing them in and stopping any hope of escape.

Not knowing where Ness and Shay are, I get out of my truck but don't approach. I know Max well enough to understand he wouldn't hesitate to use one of them as a shield from our attack. Hell, he quite possibly would kill one or both of them if only to destroy us. Even Atlas realizes the risk this represents since he has backed off the vehicle.

"Get out of the fucking truck, Maximus." I believe this won't be a seamless extraction when the doors remain closed. These lousy fuckers are going to force a fight. When the driver door flies open, I prepare myself for what I came to do, but I also release my hold on Shadow slightly in case he attempts to flee.

"Well, I have to say this isn't how I saw this going down."

"I don't give a shit how you envisioned anything. Tell me where Ness and Shay are."

"They're close." He says, directing his attention to Atlas. "Why don't you back away, big guy?"

"Not going to fucking happen," Atlas calmly replies.

"If you want to find the girls, you will back the fuck away from my truck. In fact, why don't you join us back here so we can have a conversation without anyone worrying about what the other party is doing." Atlas looks at me, and when I nod, he moves slowly around the truck until he stands beside me. With Atlas now at a safe distance in Max's mind, he moves to lean against the tailgate of his vehicle.

"How'd you find me?"

"This isn't a fucking give and take. Tell me where the girls are."

"I told you… close."

"How close?"

"You know Foster, you're a lucky man, and so are you, Brady. Ness and Shay are…" he pauses, contemplating his next words. As a cocky grin tips the side of his mouth, I prepare myself for whatever he came up with to piss us off. "delightful."

"This wasn't what I expected."

"I'm not the asshole you think I am."

"I beg to differ," Brady snarls.

"That's because I beat your ass," Max laughs, and I have to force Brady to stay put.

"I don't understand how you figured out who Shay was."

"That's simple. I was talking to my brother and mentioned there was a lovely, ravishing, utterly delectable—"

"Don't say another fucking word about your opinion of my mate. I asked you how you figured it out, and those are the only goddamn words I want to hear spilling over your useless lips."

He grins as a wicked glint flashes through his eyes. I just gave him ammunition for the only thing he can use against me, "I wonder if Shay would think my lips were useless if I was buried between those luscious thighs—"

Rushing forward, fully intent on ripping his throat out until Brady and Atlas stop me. Once Atlas has me calm again, he turns to deliver a warning of his own, "If you open your mouth and one more word about her comes tumbling out, I will rip your balls off and feed them to you before anyone realizes I moved. Are we clear on this?"

"Perfectly."

"Wonderful, as you were saying, only without the extra commentary this time."

With a grin still plastered on his face, he finishes, "Young woman who was ruining my plans, but it wasn't until I said her name that my half-wit brother put two and two together. When I snapped a picture of her and sent it to him, he was practically panting with excitement to know where he could find her again. It seems he wasn't done playing with her yet."

Pushing past them, I rush him only to be yanked away again by the men who came with me.

"I promise you will be on your knees begging for your pathetic life before this is over."

"Or on my knees, pleasing that sweet mate of yours as she begs me not to stop." No one is fast enough to stop me this time as I rush forward, slamming my fist against his jaw.

Max laughs as he mutters, "Now-now, Foster, if you hope to see them again, you will let me go."

234

I do the impossible… I back away from this fucker, knowing his threat is real. He won't tell us where to find Shay and Ness if we don't play this game by his rules.

"Oh, I suppose I should tell you I killed your mom, Brady. Sorry, man, but she had it coming."

Brady sucks in a loud breath as he starts in his direction, but my hand on his arm halts him before he can kill the only wolf who can tell us where they are.

"I can't imagine you're surprised by this confession. After all, Adela was kind of a bitch. But who am I talking to? Of course, you already knew that. How could you not with all those collars she had displayed on her wall? Disgraceful. Did you know she wrote the names of the wolves she slapped the collar on across the back?"

"If you think I believe anything you have to say, you're sadly fucking mistaken," Brady snaps.

"You can pretend all you want, but you know she was a sadistic bitch. I mean, look what she did to her own son. Do you know what surprised me the most? The fact she didn't use the same collar twice. Imagine my surprise to find Shay's name recorded on four of them."

"Bullshit."

"Not bullshit. I counted the fuckin things. Trust me, there were four." If I didn't know any better, I would say he was pissed off about what Adela did to Shay.

"I am going to rip your fucking throat out," Brady snarls.

"Well, it would be fitting since I snapped her fucking neck when I discovered collar number five." My eyes snap over to Brady, and if I didn't see anguish filling his eyes, realizing what Max just said is true and how much Shay suffered because of it, I would have applauded the prick I still plan on killing.

"Tell me where they are."

"I'll make you a deal... a life for a life."

"You think I'm letting you walk away from this?"

"I have a fairly good assumption. So what do you say? Do you want one mate, both mates, or no mates?" He's back to leaning against the tailgate. I look over at Brady because he has more invested in this choice than I do since he has a mate to consider, but he also lost his best friend, beta, and Pack. So as much as I want to take the deal to save Shay, I have to let my brother make this call. He damn well better make the right one.

"Deal."

"Excellent," he says, dragging the damn word out as he claps his hands together. "Now, don't anyone get jumpy. I just need to grab something from the back seat."

He is at least smart enough not to turn his back on us. Not that anyone would attack him, not as long as he withholds the whereabouts of Ness and Shay from us. When I see what he went to extract, Atlas has to restrain me once again.

Shay was in the fucking truck the entire time, but when I take in the state of her dress, I lose control. Had Atlas not been there, no one could have stopped me from tearing this fucker apart.

"I did tell you she was close."

"Is Ness in there too?" Brady asks as he takes a step in Max's direction.

He clicks his tongue before shattering all hope this is over. "Sadly, no. I can confirm she is also not far from here, but if you want her back in one piece, you might want to get to her before Travis does."

*****

Max

I knew I didn't stand a snowball's chance in hell of making it out of here with Shay and my life intact once they surrounded me, especially with Atlas here. Thankfully, Shay is sleeping on the backseat as she continues recovering from the abuse Adela inflicted on her.

I would have liked to have seen if I could make her fall in love with me. Not that I wanted a mate, just the challenge of winning her over. She is beautiful though. For the briefest moment, as I watch her sleep, I consider slamming my foot on the accelerator and taking my chances that I can outrun them.

But in the end, I know it is not what she wants, so I move away from the fantasy of the shy blonde-haired, blue-eyed beauty riding off in the sunset with me to getting out of here with my ass intact.

When Foster charged me, I thought he would sense Shay in the back seat; nothing would have stopped him from killing me once he had her. If it hadn't been for the time she spent in the collar, he would have, but with her wolf on hiatus, it made it harder for him to do this.

With Foster and Brady's promise to release me, I retrieve the first of the women they seek.

"I need you to wake up, kitten."

"Are we back already?"

"Nope, but I do have a surprise for you." Her sleepy eyes flutter open as I help her slide out of the backseat. The air she sucks in when she sees Foster tells me I never stood a chance of winning shit with her. I guess the mate bond really is as strong as they claim.

Marcelle Valentine

"Foster," she whispers. Relief, followed by rage, covers his face when he sees her standing here in nothing but my coat. I could have kept my shit and left her nude, but I felt that might be awkward for all parties involved.

"It looks like I found his weakness. Such a fucking shame he didn't realize I could never hurt you either." Foster's eyes burn with hate as he watches me whispering in her ear.

"I would never hurt such a delicious beauty. I want you to know why I wouldn't allow Travis to touch you. It's because I wanted to be the one sliding between those silky thighs, but I had no intention of doing it by force. I wanted to hear all the sexy sounds I know you are capable of producing. The thing is, I wanted them to come from you willingly." Shay's eyes snap to mine, and I take a second to soak up the beauty I find in them since this is the last time I will ever see them.

I am not a dumb man. Foster may have given me his word to let me go, but that doesn't mean he won't want to hunt me down. When I hear Foster growl, I know our time is done.

"Do you remember how to get back to the house where Ness is?"

"I think so."

"Then you better hurry, kitten, because my brother didn't like me taking his prize from him, and I'm afraid Ness won't be as lucky," I say, backing away from Shay.

When Foster moves, so do I as I jump into my truck to peel away, hoping to put as much distance as possible between myself and these men who want to kill me. Here's hoping they want to save Ness more than end me.

238

Episode One-Hundred Twenty-Three: Is This the End

Shay

I SUPPOSE THIS story started with me, so it seems fitting for it to end with me.

My entire life, I have been able to hide who I am. Shrinking back until I am damn near invisible. But Foster doesn't allow me to do this. Not anymore. I feel seen, heard, and loved for the first time. With him, I have never felt more alive. I can lie to everyone else around me, but I cannot lie to the man who stole my heart. He is everything I have ever needed and will forever be the only man I ever want.

I know Foster is still searching for Max, and while I don't think he should walk away from what he did scot-free, I struggle knowing he protected me when Foster and I couldn't. In many ways, I know it is only because of Max that I left that situation, the same woman I was when I walked in. While also understanding, but for his actions, I never would have found myself in the damn thing to begin with. I have only told Foster and Ness this because I know Brady and Maggie will never understand, nor will they forgive him for what he did to Colton. I just don't have it in me to hate him. So, for the peace of our pack, I keep my thoughts to myself.

The day Max left me in the middle of the road, we raced to where I knew Ness was waiting for her miracle. For her mate Brady to save her. If we had arrived any later, Travis would have had the time to take his frustration out on this beautiful soul. He would have brutalized Ness without a second thought. Unlike Max, Travis had nothing to bargain with, so his death was sealed the second Brady found him hovering over his mate.

When we returned to the pack, Foster told me I could have all the time I needed, but I didn't want time... I needed him. And while I'm still not convinced I'll make a good Luna, I will try every day to show the wolves who count on me that I am a person they can count on and trust.

It seems Finn found the same thing with Sadie that Maggie did with Colton. They are happy and hope that whoever their true mates are, they find the same love they did because neither one plans to accept another wolf. I suppose they made this clear after they had their own marking ceremony.

It overjoyed Aunt Claire to see all her kids happy, in love, and planning their future. She once told me she was terrified Foster would remain alone for the rest of his life. Claire was afraid he would never get over the loss of his mom or forget what happened to Fay. She thanks the Moon Goddess every day I left my pack behind because it brought me to him, and if anyone deserved to find happiness, it was Foster and me. I almost cried the first time she introduced me as her future daughter. Not a niece, not a daughter-in-law. Her daughter and being someone's daughter is something I never thought I would have again. Oh, and it pleases all of us that Ian finally worked up enough nerve to ask Aunt Claire out.

Maggie is still learning how to live without Colton in her world. She asked Ness to teach her how to be a Salutary. I don't know if she plans to follow Seamus and never take another mate. I hope this is not her path, but if it is, I'll be there to support her every step of the way.

Ian stepped down as Beta as soon as we returned. Foster initially asked Finn, and had I not been present, I'm not sure I would have believed Foster's rendition because Finch denies everything, saying it never happened before he winks at me.

"Don't look at me, bro; I enjoy being free. I'm an independent man."

"Who the hell said you won't still be independent, Finn? Being the beta doesn't mean you're married to the pack."

"Bullshit," he interrupts. "Because that is precisely what it means. My life will no longer be my own. It belongs to the pack, and right now, there is only one wolf I want to belong to. I know someone you could ask though."

"Brady will never agree to be my Beta. He's the alpha of his own pack."

"Brady doesn't want to lead, and he doesn't want to leave Lake because this is where Nessie feels the happiest. That man will do anything to ensure she smiles for the rest of her life."

To Foster, mine, and just about everyone else's astonishment, Brady happily accepts the beta position. He can say that Alpha's life wasn't cut out for him all he wanted; I know the truth. He did this for Ness, and she could not be happier with his choice. Shortly after Brady announced he wouldn't return to Half Crest, Ash Rock picked up several new members, including Ophelia and Rose, who were happy they no longer had to hide their relationship. They plan to adopt a pup discovered in the woods recently. A little girl with beautiful green eyes.

We're planning Brady and Ness's wedding for late fall. She said she wanted it to be the last celebration of the season. Foster was happy to hear she didn't plan on having it at his cottage. I know I've said this already, but it's as true now as it was then. I cannot believe how much my life has changed.

Riona thankfully disappeared shortly after Atlas left town. Not sure where she went or what's going on with him, but he promised he would be back, and thankfully he chose today to be the day he returned, which is a good thing since Foster and I are getting married this afternoon.

"He's not a shifter, is he?"

"No, he's not."

"But he's not human either. I can sense something is different about him, yet I can't put my finger on it."

"I will confirm he is not human."

"But you're not going to tell me what he is, are you?"

"Not my story to tell, beautiful."

"Come on, Foss, how are we supposed to be partners if we keep things from each other?"

"Anything else, my beautiful Luna, but not this."

"Why?"

"Because my friend is trying to uphold a promise he made."

I spin around to find Atlas lounging against the doorframe.

"Okay, so how about you tell me?"

"Of course, I'll tell the mate of one of my best friends and the Luna of this pack."

Ness and I do a lousy job pretending to patiently wait for him to make his confession, which causes him and Denver to laugh.

"Oh, for shit's sake, Atlas, what are you?" I can't keep my excitement from seeping into my question.

"My father is the king of the fae. Which makes me—"

"A fucking fae prince," Ness squeals.

"While I prefer to leave the fucking part out, yes, I am a fae prince."

"Holy shit on a stick. We've been surrounded by royalty this whole time."

"It's not something Atlas talks about," Denver says as he nudges his shoulder.

"Are you royalty too, Denver?" Ness asks.

"I can confirm he's a royal pain in my ass," Atlas laughs.

"Nope, just the lifelong friend and bodyguard of one."

"I've always wondered if fairies existed."

"Fae and fairies are two different things."

"How so?"

"Fae is a race of people. Fairies are something normal mortals made up to grant wishes to future princesses," He tells me as he taps my nose.

After everyone returns to the reception, Atlas asks Foster and me for a favor. He tells us his dad took a turn for the worse, and if he has any hope of finding Ayaan, the asshole responsible for his ailing father, he needs to go now, but he can't take Denver with him because the Vanguard is hot on their trail. He also doesn't want him to stay in Lake since the sweeps through here have increased exponentially, thanks to Max and Travis. Yet another reason everyone hates him.

Foster seems to have an alternative. He tells Atlas he can hide Denver in our sister pack, Whispering Winds. One of his best friends is there, and he can assure Atlas Denver will be safe and welcome there.

Marcelle Valentine

Later, my handsome mate must tell me about this secret best friend, Archer. For now, I know he lived within this pack until he was fourteen when his mom met a wolf from Whispering Winds. Since they were already sister packs, the Alphas happily agreed with Archer's mom's petition to switch groups, but Foster and Archer remained close.

As the evening winds down on our wedding reception, I ask my husband to dance with me. I have something he has yet to find, but I have little doubt he will discover it with this simple request.

He takes my hand to lead me out to the center of the room, my heart racing as warmth spreads through my body. The way Foster holds me close to him, his hand on the small of my back, sends shivers running down my spine. As he whispers his dirty sexy intentions in my ear, his breath on my neck produces goosebumps all over my trembling frame.

I can see the desire in his eyes, and I know he feels the same way I do. The anticipation of what is coming is almost too much to bear. My body responds to his masterful touch, and I know he can also sense my increasing excitement.

As the song ends, Foster pulls me close and dips me low, his lips capturing mine in a passionate kiss. Fireworks explode inside me as his tongue caresses mine, and I know this is just the beginning of a long, sensual night. As his hands slide from my waist to my hips, I can feel the anticipation of the coming night.

"What are you wearing, beautiful?" he asks when his hands discovers what I've hidden from him all day. This is when I'm sure he found the gift I want him to unwrap.

With my knowing grin tipping my lips at what he just encountered, I wait for what I know is coming. Did I do this intentionally? You bet your ass I did because it guarantees he'll kick everyone out so he can remove them. I wouldn't be opposed to him doing this with his teeth. When I bite my lip and shrug one shoulder while looking up at him through my lashes, his grin is decadent and delicious in all the ways that send heat racing through me and pooling to the spot I want him kissing... making his grin turn positively sinful.

"Everyone get the fuck out," Foster says as he slides his hand under my dress, brushing his fingers over the clit, awaiting his kiss and skillful teasing tongue.

"I love you, babe," I tell him as my hand reaches into his pants to stroke his magical cock.

"As much as I love you, beautiful," he tells me as I press my lips to his while he finally slides away the thin swath of material he finds utterly offensive.

At this moment, nothing in the world exists except Foster and me, our bodies entwined in a dance of desire. I know we have a lifetime of passion ahead of us, and I am grateful for every moment we share. But I need my husband to satiate the building fire between my legs.

As he kisses me again, his lips taste like the champagne we've been drinking all night. The surge of desire coursing through my body to take him right here in the middle of the dance floor is the only thought consuming me. I want him more than anything, but he wants me just as much.

He lifts me like I'm nothing to carry me to the table where we shared our first meal as husband and wife. I can feel the softness of the linens against my skin when he tears the dress concealing my body from his touch. I wrap my arms around his neck, pulling him close while he makes short work of removing the offending garment and keeping him from his goal.

As he explores my body with his hands and mouth, every nerve ending in it comes alive with desire. I arch my back, moaning his name. He responds by taking me to new heights of ecstasy.

Foster's tongue circles my clit like he was born to do this, and I can't help but arch my back and grip the edge of the table. The sound of his low groans mixed with my moans fills the room, and I can feel the heat rising between us.

Our breathing fills the air, each gasp and moan a testament to the pleasure we're experiencing. I can feel the coolness of the air on my skin and the heat of Foster's mouth against my pussy, already burning from my desire.

The smell of sex and sweat is thick in the air, but it only adds to the intensity of the moment. I'm on the brink of ecstasy as the slickness intensifies, coating my thighs and his lips.

I gasp when Foster's fingers slip inside me as he hits the one spot he knows will send me reeling. He knows my body better than I thought possible, and I can't imagine being with anyone else.

At the height of my orgasm, I release a loud cry, and Foster's name spills from my lips. Yet he doesn't stop until I'm spent.

This is how my story ends with my husband on his knees, pleasuring me while I scream his name. If I had known this was the life I could have, I would have left a hell of a lot sooner. I wouldn't have been so fucking terrified of being rogue, broke, or alone in the world. I would have embraced my future, knowing the Goddess would put me right where I was always meant to be. In Lake, where my family was waiting patiently for me, but more importantly, right here in the arms of the man I have given my heart to.

And this thought alone fills me with a sense of utter bliss when I drop to my knees and push him against the table so I can run my tongue along his shaft while Foster, my mate, my husband, the man who pledged their life to us, looks at me like I'm the only woman in the world.

Note from the Author: I hope you enjoyed meeting the gang of Ash Rock. Next up is our Fae Prince Atlas's story. He has to find Ayaan, save his dad, and figure out who betrayed them all while trying not to fall for the girl helping him. The Ash Rock gang might occasionally pop up in his story, and a certain Alpha-chasing Irish troublemaking Riona will return since she has set her sights on a new man. Atlas's story will release on Vella first but will come to Kindle, Kindle Unlimited, and paperback approximately thirty days after I have completed each season on Vella. If you are interested in following Atlas's story, check him out in his story Silverwood Throne: Return of the Fae Prince releasing now on Kindle Vella.

Also by *Marcelle Valentine*

Scarred by Fate Series
Ritual Nightmare
Breaking Purgatory
Fate's Ritual
Opposing Tartarus
Sacrificial Endings

The Ash Rock Series
Shadow's Moon Season One
Shadow's Moon Season Two
Shadow's Moon Season Three
Shadow's Moon Season Four

Arrival of the Four Horsemen Series
Death's Inquest
Pestilence's Judgment
War's Verdict
Coming Soon Famine's Punishment

Kindle Vella
Shadow's Moon Season One through Four
Seized by Sin
Silverwood Throne

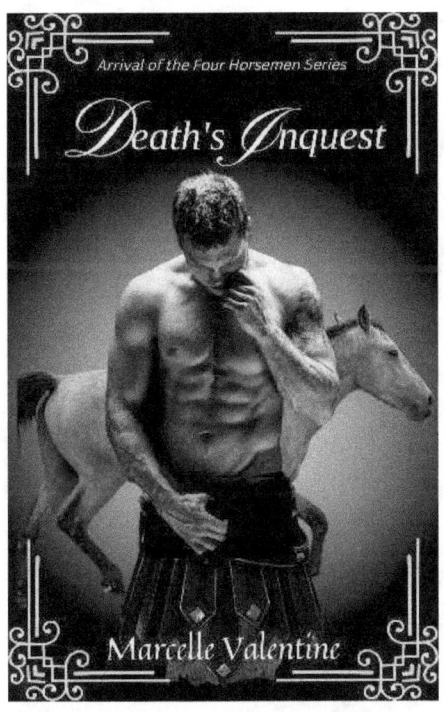

Teaser

What do you do when you meet a fabled rider of the Apocalypse?

In my case, nurse him back to health, and hope like hell I can outrun him. Yet the whole outrunning him plan is proving to be more difficult than expected.

Especially when the good and honorable men in the city I'm hiding in decide the only way to save themselves is to give the rider a tribute. It seems I'm to be the unlucky sacrificial lamb they selected.

But why would I expect anything less since my life has never been easy? It's been one trial after another, yet they served a purpose. It's only because of these lessons I have the strength to stand rather than cower. Even when the one I face is the rider sent to determine our worth.

As his decision becomes clear, humanity will fall. I do something no sane person would... I proposition the rider. He promises to leave us in peace if I can prove our worth. The longer we travel together, it becomes increasingly difficult to deny my growing attraction, and a new fear begins. Is it possible I have met the only being who will accomplish what none of the others have ever managed to do.... Could Thanatos be the one to finally break me?

Has Avalon discovered the one who can change everything, or will her fears prove true? Grab your copy of Death's Inquest to follow Avalon's journey.

Acknowledgments

I don't know how you feel, but this has been one hell of a ride. As you may know, the gang of Ash Rock was only supposed to be a short novella. A one and done story so I could try out Kindle Vella, and it morphed into four seasons with at least one planned spin-off. I hope you have enjoyed getting to know these characters as much as I have enjoyed writing them. The good news is they may pop up periodically in Atlas's story. Which if everything has come to plan is already releasing on Kindle Vella.

The biggest thanks need to go out to all my readers who decided to travel with me on this journey. Each book of mine that you read is another chance for me to take you to hidden worlds filled with wondrous mysteries and alpha men.

I could not have completed this without those who supported me, including my beta readers, my niece Ashley, my mom, and my daughter Melanie. I could never say thank you enough for everything you each did to help me bring this project to life.

Book four in my Arrival of the Four Horsemen is well underway and should be released in 2023.

Thank you to my husband and everyone else in my family who have been my biggest cheerleaders. I love each and every one of you.

And finally, to every author that has ever put pen to paper, fingers to keyboard, whose work only inspired me more to follow this dream, I hope I do not disappoint.

Thank you
Marcelle

Newsletter

Consider visiting my website and signing up for my newsletter to receive updates on this series and future projects.

https://marcellevalentine.com/books

If you enjoyed the book, please consider leaving a review wherever you purchase your books. Any thoughts are appreciated and will only help me improve the stories. Reviews also provide new readers with a way to find my books.
You can also follow me on social media.

Facebook
Goodreads
Instagram
TikTok

About the Author

Marcelle Valentine has long been an admirer of creating worlds in which people can get lost in. From the time when she was little, her active imagination took her on epic journeys to faraway places where troubles and friendships abound. Discovering Paranormal and Fantasy Romance books brought back memories of old friends and magical realms, reigniting her passion for writing. She invites you to travel with her during these journeys and get lost in a world where you will find friends, enemies, and lovers all waiting to whisk you away. Marcelle is the author of the Scarred by Fate Series, Arrival of the Four Horsemen Pentalogy, and the episodic series Shadow's Moon. She lives in Ohio with her husband. She has two children, three grandchildren, and one lovable, lazy Great Dane.

Marcellevalentine.com

Facebook

Goodreads

Instagram

TikTok